THE HOLE IN THE BONE

J. Thomas Brown

FENGHUANG PUBLISHING

First published 2018 by FENGHUANG PUBLISHING

ISBN 978-0-578-40027-3 (Paperback)
ISBN 978-1-5323-9628-1 (ebook)

To connect with the author please visit www.jthomasbrown.com

Acknowledgements

Much credit is due to my son for his help with little-known behind-the-scenes museum practices and in the handling and transportation of relics and human remains. "Thank you, Justin, the story would not have been possible without you."

Chapter One:

The Blue Baby

NICK CLIMBED THE STAIRS two at a time, then race-walked down the hallway to the Department of Ancient Studies, late again. Unnoticed, he slunk into his office, plonked down at the computer, and entered his password. A message flashed on the screen: YOUR PASSWORD HAS EXPIRED.

Gail poked her head in the door. "Don't forget there's a meeting."

"I know."

Nick followed Gail into the conference room and sat down beside her at a long, oval table where thirty other archaeologists, artisans, and museum staff were already seated. Gail Norton was tall and physically fit from the demanding labor of archaeological excavations, although her tan had faded long before.

She leaned toward Nick and smiled. "A crate came addressed to you this morning. Security asked me where it should go since you weren't in yet."

"What is it?" he asked.

"It's a mummy. An infant, from China. Probably very old. It needs carbon dating."

Nothing interesting had come his way since he was called in from the field a year ago. He sat up straight. "Where in China?"

"Someplace called Shamadù in Xinjiang. There were some artifacts with it. A baby bottle made from an udder stretched over a horn, a blanket, and some blue stones."

Dr. John Mohr, the department head, walked in and stood at the head of the table. He began explaining that the department's budget had been cut. To save money, they were changing to a new insurance provider. He nodded to the HR administrator who started droning off a list of changes.

Nick's mind wandered to the excavation he worked on in Peru two years before. He had requested to return there several times, but Mohr, his boss, never approved his reassignment. Instead, he was kept inside to research and cross-reference artifacts for the department head's forthcoming book, a catalogue of pre-Columbian art. He felt himself growing drowsy.

Gail nudged Nick in the side when his head fell forward. He straightened upright and looked at her wistfully. She often talked about her last project in Ife, Nigeria and seemed to share his feeling of being buried alive in paperwork and academic pablum. Another bleak day of typing up indexes, headings, and bullets stretched ahead.

"Nick. Did you finish those indexes yet?" Mohr called

out across the room as everyone filed out after the meeting.

"I'll email them to you this afternoon," said Nick, disappearing through the door behind Gail. When he returned to his office, there was a message to contact the administrator, so Nick called the help desk. The person who answered explained that the technical staff was in a meeting. Confinement wasn't his bailiwick. To be an archaeologist, you had to get out of the office.

Remembering the mummy, he dialed Gail's extension. "Did you have security send the crate to screening?"

"I can meet you there in five minutes," she said.

The DSA, designated screening area, was in the basement. Artifacts were quarantined there until they could be verified there were no contaminants that would jeopardize the existing collections. From there, items were cataloged and dispersed to other locations or placed in storage in the basement, where artifacts from all over the world stretched in a labyrinth of shelves and cabinets to the back of the building.

The door lock responded to Nick's fingerprint. Inside, Gail pointed to a wooden box on a workbench. On the front a label read: Infant Caucasian Mummy, Shamadù, Xinjiang Autonomous Region.

"There's no tamper tape," he remarked.

Gail shook her head. "It didn't come through the usual channels." She handed him a shipping form. "It's from a Chinese art gallery in Beijing. Don't ask me how they got it through customs."

Together they lifted the lid. Gail took several photos, then removed a layer of cheesecloth from the box, exposing several large packs of silica gel and bundling soaked in a pesticide that smelled like mothballs. She handed Nick the camera and then began to carefully remove the final protective layer. When the last remnant of cloth was gone, Nick took several more photos and moved a directional light closer to the box to look inside.

He had a sensation of floating through space and time as he peered down at the child's face. Its serene countenance looked back through two polished blue stones affixed to the empty eye sockets. The expression seemed to say it had been to the beyond and had found the answer to the riddle of that other world but remained bound to an unbreakable code of silence.

The infant was swaddled in a blue blanket. Nick reached down and gingerly brushed the wool with the back of his hand, feeling its softness despite the latex gloves he wore. He grasped the feeding horn lying beside the corpse and set it on the workbench.

"I've never seen one in such good condition. These remains aren't mummified. They're desiccated. Egyptian mummies look ready to crumble, but not this. It's a different technique. It looks almost alive, and there's no discoloration." He leaned against Gail, peering in closer. "What do you think the infant died of?"

"We could examine the internal bones and organs with an MRI."

Nick straightened. "Are you thinking what I'm thinking?"

Gail smiled playfully. "Are you sure you want to know?"

He looked back into the crate, reddening. "I mean, you know Mohr's not going to approve. What did he say when you told him about this?"

"He was too busy for me to tell him. Every time I get near him he's on the phone about his book."

Nick outlined a course of action. "If we don't get started now it could end up on the shelves here forever. I'll order two carbon date tests: a beta on the horn material and an AMS on the infant. If the dates are close, the results will be valid. I might as well sign for the MRI too."

"He'll be royally pissed off with his budget cuts. The MRI is my idea, let me sign for it," she insisted.

Nick wanted her to think he was more than just a lackey for the head of the department. "I'll sign. He's already pissed off with me anyway."

They agreed to lunch at a deli across the street. After ordering their food they found a table. "It seems like there's something missing about the whole mummy thing," said Gail.

Nick nodded. "I know. Like it's more than a stroke of luck." He offered her his pickle.

Gail accepted and took a bite. "It doesn't make sense. If it was found in Xinjiang, why was it sent from an art gallery in Beijing?"

"A lot of mummies have been found in the Taklamakan Desert in Xinjiang. The extremes of temperature have a freeze-drying effect and some cultures used that to preserve their dead. The Xinjiang part makes sense. But it's illegal to send human remains overseas without transport forms. Someone wanted to avoid red tape ... and detection."

She shoved the mustard across the table. "You should have seen the expression on your face when you looked inside the crate."

"It was a weird feeling, like deja vu. Those blue stones remind me of something, but I'm not sure what. We have to get in touch with the art gallery. I have lots of questions."

Chapter Two:

Weijii

AFTER NICK GOT BACK to his office, the phone rang. "How are you, Nick? We've been out of touch too long."

It had been a few years, but Nick recognized the voice as that of his college roommate, Michael Chou, who still spoke English with hints of an underlying Cantonese regiolect.

"Michael, I can't believe it's you. What are you doing now?"

"I'm the director of the Regional Museum of Xinjiang. There is so much to tell you. Too much to talk about over phone. We must meet right away. There are some big things going on in Xinjiang."

"It's coming together. Did you send the mummy?"

"I meant to call you sooner. I can't believe you got it so fast. My wife had the idea to send it as art instead of human remains."

"So, you're married. Congratulations."

Michael laughed. "For two years, my friend."

"Anyone I know?"

"No. Her name is Ann Lee. She's an art dealer and has a gallery in Beijing and one in Manhattan. She helped me send the mummy over to you to try to come in the back door, so to speak. Otherwise it would take months to get it to you with all the red tape. I'm trying to create interest in some of the new finds we have made in Shamadù. They are going to change the history books. Several new settlements were discovered buried by the dried-up lakebeds below Loulan."

Nick swiveled his seat around to face his corkboard. The map of Asia was covered over with post-its and catalogue numbers on index cards. "That's along the Old Silk Road, isn't it?"

"Yes, Southeastern Xinjiang. The problem is, we still don't have enough backing to explore or excavate."

"The word around here is that the well is dry. I might be able to swing a speaking slot for you, if you're interested."

"That is what I'm hoping for. Listen, Nick, there are people who think they will get rich selling relics on the black market and are destroying much historical evidence. We need to get there first. We are short on equipment and funds and need international collaboration. I can explain better in person. Ann Lee and I are in New York for a couple of weeks. How about if she and I come down to see you tomorrow? We can have dinner together and catch up."

Nick glanced at his empty calendar. "I'm available. I'll find us a good place to eat. I'm going to ask a colleague of mine to come." They agreed on eight o'clock.

Nick returned to the DSA and got started on the carbon dating. Taking a small half-ounce chip from the underside of the horn, he brought it to the lab on the second floor. After a beta analysis, the result indicated 3,803 years, give or take about eight years in either direction. He whistled to himself and checked the procedure to make certain it was accurate.

The second test was to be made on the mummy itself and was more involved. He brought in a lab assistant and called Gail and asked her to help. They tried to unwrap the freeze-dried infant from the blue blanket it was tightly bound in but became fearful of damaging the limbs. Gail made a small incision through the combed wool with a scalpel, then another through the parchment of skin stretched over an inner thigh. Using retractors, she opened the incision and parted the lips of the brittle wound to expose the bone. Nick sliced off a flake with a microtome, then the lab assistant picked up the sample with tweezers and deposited it into a vial.

They brought the specimen back to the lab and set up the accelerator mass spectrometer for the final test. The AMS filled half the lab; the accelerator chamber portion nearly reached the ceiling. After the bone sample had been analyzed, the results were plugged into a computer to determine when the once living material had ceased to absorb carbon-14. The result would indicate the age to within a few percentage points. If the sample from the horn and the bone were reasonably close, there would be an even greater indication that the tests were yielding accurate results. After running through the procedure twice to be sure, they had their answer: 3,798 years.

Gail's eyes popped. "That's the Xia dynasty."

"What's so special about the Xia dynasty?" asked the lab assistant.

Gail placed the printout of the test results in a bin along with the sample vial. "It was the beginning of rule by families of hereditary kings. The Xia kings were shamanic rulers who communicated with spirits and read oracle bones. They ruled by dramatic demonstrations of their power over their subjects. Legend has it that Emperor Xia Jie made three thousand people drown themselves by jumping into a lake of wine."

The lab assistant shook his head in disbelief. "That's a lot of clout, but maybe it's not a bad way to go." He toggled off a bank of switches on the AMS, and the room got quiet.

Nick took off his lab coat and threw it on a stool nearby. "You have an excellent point. It beats torture or having your head cut off." He rolled up his sleeves and sat down to type the results into a computer. "Things got better. In time, the ancient Chinese came to believe that if a ruler violated the principles of good government, the dynasty would end by something called the Mandate of Heaven. That's what happened to Jie. He was violently overthrown by the Shangs. The only Xia king to survive was Xie Pu who died of old age a few years later in Xinjiang."

There were no windows in the lab, and Gail had lost track of time. "I didn't realize how late it is. I hate to run out on you now, but there's a seminar on satellite imaging at Widener Hall tonight, and I'm leading the panel discussion. I'm heading out." She hung her lab coat on the hook by the door and threw her gloves into the medical waste bin. "Goodnight."

It was ten p.m. by the time Nick finished entering the tests into the logs and documenting the results. He stretched and walked over to the remains of the infant which they had begun to refer to as "the Blue Baby."

"I've got a wife and kids, Doc," said the technician. "I'm getting out of here."

"I really appreciate your staying late. Blame it on me to your wife."

Nick waited for the door to close, then stared intently at the blue stones, trying to remember why they were familiar. After drawing a blank, he turned out the lights and walked wearily to the elevator, wondering what tomorrow's MRI would show.

☙

Nick got home late and went straight to bed. Sleep came quickly, but his limbs were restless, and he tossed repeatedly. In short clips of motion and brief snatches of conversation, the day's events passed on his closed eyelids. Eventually the deeper layers were reached, and his muscles lost tension. He traveled to the world of inner space and began dreaming in vivid color.

He was a pedestrian on a crowded city walkway. Screams filled the air as a black SUV came barreling over the curb, running people down on the sidewalk. He tried to jump clear but was struck on the side and thrown through the air, landing him in complete darkness. A glowing figure unfolded in front of him, until it solidified and took the shape of a tall man. He was dressed in a dark maroon waistcoat with matching leggings and bright woolen shanks that hung over the tops of deerskin boots. His face and hands were covered with intricate tattoos. He advanced slowly, speaking a foreign language the dreamer could somehow understand, saying not to be afraid, that they had something in common.

Nick tried to raise his hands but couldn't move. As the tall man stepped closer, he extended his right arm and thrust a hand through Nick's skin and deep inside the internal organs. Nick felt a suction as the hand groped through his spleen and pushed against the lower ribs. The man grasped a rib, then snapped it off and pulled it out from the side, holding up the short, bloody bone. He lifted the rib to eyelevel, then turned it sideways, revealing a hole in the middle.

As Nick looked through, shapes formed on the other side. The dream invader regarded Nick with a broad smile and reinserted it back into the opening from which it came.

Nick fought the sleep paralysis and brought himself to wakefulness. He was clammy and shaking. His side burned as he forced himself to replay the dream in his head.

Despite the unrestful sleep and the unsolved mystery from inner space, Nick rose with a bolt of anticipation and left for work ahead of time. He started his car and pulled out of the parking space in front of his apartment thinking he would be early. As he drove down the street to make the same turn he made every morning, a black SUV was approaching to cross the intersection. Nick arrived first and began turning, but his assumption that the other vehicle would stop was wrong. The front bumper hit his door, caving it in and slamming the armrest into his ribs. Both vehicles skidded to a halt. The SUV was barely scratched, but the trim and mirror were torn from the side of Nick's car and dangled by a thread. A nasty pain throbbed in his side and he had to take a couple of deep breaths to get it under control.

The drivers got out and inspected the damage. After exchanging information, Nick pulled out his cell phone and took pictures, then the SUV drove away. Nick slammed his door several times to make it stay closed, then resumed his way to work.

The pain in his side couldn't be ignored, and he decided to visit a nearby clinic. After a quick examination, he was sent to the radiology department. Several X-rays were taken in increasingly painful positions, then he was told to wait in one of the examining rooms.

Half an hour later, a doctor walked through the curtains. "Sorry to make you wait so long. We're having the equipment checked."

Nick held his breath and squinted as he pushed himself up straight on the gurney. "What's wrong? I really need to get to work."

"It's a routine check of the calibration. It won't be long." The doctor disappeared back through the curtains.

Nick spent the next ten minutes wishing he hadn't left his cell phone in his car. Finally, the radiology technician entered. "Just one more time. I'm really sorry." He walked Nick back to radiology and repeated the painful procedure.

"We have the results," the physician told him a short while later. "You have a crack in one of your lower ribs. You're going to be sore for a few weeks."

"So my rib is broken, not the X-ray machine? Are you going to tape it?"

"No. Not for the small ribs. There's little we can do. It'll heal on its own. There is something interesting. You have twenty-five ribs. Most people have only twenty-four."

Nick's eyebrows raised an inch. "I have an extra rib?"

The physician nodded. "Everyone has lower small ribs that don't go all the way around the front. They're called floating ribs. You have an extra floating rib. It doesn't interfere with anything, but there's no biological purpose to it." He held up the X-ray and pointed with his pen. "This is the break, right here, on the nineteenth. And this is the twenty-fifth."

"What's that?" asked Nick, stabbing his finger at a dark spot on the extra rib.

"Just a speck of dust on the lens."

∾

He arrived at 11:30, breaking all previous records for lateness. When he caught up with Gail in her office she looked at him reproachfully. "Where have you been all morning?"

"I was in an accident."

"You should have called. I was worried."

"Sorry." He bit his lip

She filled him in on the morning's events. "I ran the MRI and looked over the images from the scans. There aren't any obvious signs of foul play, but we still don't know the cause of death."

"Perhaps the mother died first, then the infant starved."

"That could be. Oh, I almost forgot. Guess who was looking for you?"

"Mohr?"

"He didn't look happy."

Nick grimaced as he turned to go. "He never does."

Dr. John Mohr had the largest of all the offices. Statues and relics were carefully placed throughout the room to strike the eye from the perspective of those seated in front of his massive oak desk. A life-sized statue of Horus loomed behind, staring over Mohr's shoulder into infinity.

"Better shut the door," Mohr said.

Nick closed the door and sat down, sagging through the seat cushion halfway to the floor. His cracked rib ached, but he knew something more painful than that was about to get underway.

Mohr gazed at Nick impassively. "I was trying to get in touch with you all morning. Where were you?"

Nick frowned at the thought of having to explain himself. "I was in a car accident and had to have some X-rays taken."

Mohr clasped his hands together, intertwining his fingers. "I see," he intoned, wriggling his fingers. "I didn't get your email. Is the project I gave you finished?"

"Almost. I just need a week more."

"You've been busy with your own projects. That's why you couldn't finish what you were supposed to do. You've shown a total lack of interest in what's going on here, not to mention your lateness every day, but the thing that really drives me over the edge is spending $22,000 on your own unauthorized lab tests without even discussing it with me."

The leather creaked as Nick tried to shift his position in the chair. "Those tests were for the Xinjiang mummy. There are things happening in Xinjiang that are as great as the discovery of King Tut's tomb. We tried to tell you, but you were too busy working on your own projects."

"I set the priorities, Taylor, not you. There are bigger issues that you don't even know about. What matters is that our budget has been cut in half. I can't have that much money spent on personal whims, or on people who don't carry their own weight."

"That mummy is 3,800 years old, and there are more to be found. We have got to get in on this. History is going to be rewritten. The test costs are nothing compared to the importance to archaeology."

Mohr formed a steeple with his fingers. "That's it, Taylor. You're laid off, effective immediately. HR will go over it with you."

Nick stood and leaned over Mohr's desk. He had gone too far to retreat at this point. "I'll bet most of the budget goes to publishing your own book anyway; *More of the Same* by the famous John Mohr."

"That did it. Forget about collecting unemployment. You're fired. Pack up your things, Taylor, and go. I'll have security walk you out."

Nick said quick good-byes to surprised colleagues on his way back to his office. He found some boxes and had started filling them when Gail walked in.

"The old curmudgeon bastard fired me."

"I told you he'd get mad."

Nick let the remark pass. He remembered the dinner with Michael and Ann Lee and wondered what Gail would think about going with him now. "Look, Gail, I know I'm a hothead, but it was for a good cause. A friend of mine, Michael Chou, called me yesterday. His wife is an international art dealer. She sent the Blue Baby as art to avoid customs. He wants us to have dinner with them tonight. Can you make it?"

A wistful smile flickered on her lips.

"Are you asking me out on a date?"

Before he could reply, there was a knock on his door, and two security guards entered.

"Are you ready, Mr. Taylor?" one of them asked.

"Just hold on for two more minutes, if you can, please," Nick shot back angrily.

"I'll come. Anything for the sake of science."

"I wanted to have dinner with you for a long time. I'm not asking you to further my career at the university, that's for sure." He tossed an African talking stick in the box on top a fourteen-hundred-year-old clay figurine.

"Okay. I really do want to come."

Nick beamed as security escorted him into the hall. "I'll pick you up at seven."

"You'll find something better," she called out after him.

❧

When he arrived at Gail's house she wouldn't get in his car. "We'll take mine," she said, opening her car door.

Nick had made reservations at Phillip's Seafood House, an unpretentious spot where the food was excellent. Michael spotted them as soon as they walked through the door and went to greet them.

"Hello, Nick, my friend, how are you?" Michael said, pumping Nick's arm. Ann Lee, this is Nick Taylor. My friend from college days."

"I'm so pleased to meet you, Nick," she said, smiling warmly. "Michael has been singing your praise all evening, but you don't look like the troublemaker he was telling me about."

"I doubt he's improved any since then," said Gail.

"This is Gail Norton," said Nick. "We work together at the Department of Antiquities. She's also our imaging specialist."

He checked in with the hostess who took them to a table by a window looking out on a clipper ship docked across the street at Penn's Landing. Nick waited until after they had ordered their food and chosen a wine to catch up on things.

"So, what happened after graduation, Michael? How did you end up at the Regional Museum of Xinjiang?"

"Let me start with what I would call the beginning," said Michael. "After I finished my education in the States, I went to visit relatives in Beijing. I met Ann Lee at an exhibition at her gallery. I waited until she closed for the day, then asked her out. I wouldn't leave until she said yes."

Ann Lee kissed him on the cheek. "That's the problem. No one can ever get him to leave."

Michael patted her hand. "I was going to go back to the States, but she convinced me to stay in China. I got a job with the Chinese Institute of Archeology. A few months later we were married. We moved to Urumqi, and I began my job at the museum under Dr. Lei Wang. Three years later he died of a stroke just after he turned eighty. When they offered me his position, I accepted."

"I know of Dr. Wang's work on Mount Li, the uncovering of the mausoleum of First Emperor Qin Shi Huang Di," said Gail.

Michael nodded. "He was a master detective and able to determine the location of the terracotta army by studying the ancient writings of the Shiji. We are much indebted to him."

"It's a shame to lose such a great mind," said Nick, "but what about the big things happening in Xinjiang you mentioned? How does the infant mummy tie into this?"

Michael pulled a photocopy of a newspaper article from his pocket and unfolded it on the table. "Before Dr. Wang died, he had shown me this article published over one hundred years ago by a Swedish explorer, Folkman Sorenson. An expedition, sponsored by the Swedish government and the British Museum in 1883, was organized to study the Silk Road. The locals of Shamadù talked of mummies that had been found in the desert not far from the Kunlun Mountains and led Sorenson and his team to a small tomb containing three adult mummies. All three were exceptionally well preserved and dressed in clothes of Western origin, and according to Sorenson, they were Caucasian. The expedition traveled by camel with no means to transport the remains without causing damage. They took photos and resealed the tomb. I spent a year trying to relocate it, but the desert sands shift and move all the time. I couldn't find it, but I did find the infant mummy. It was sealed in a boat covered with ox hide in a depression between the dunes. That tomb is waiting to be rediscovered."

"What would Caucasians be doing there?" said Nick.

"Maybe the Silk Road was in use earlier than we think. There are many cultures living in the Xinjiang region today. Why couldn't there have been Caucasians there a long time ago? In any event, we won't find answers until we bring in more expertise and build an international effort."

"There must be a permanent settlement of some kind nearby if they went to the trouble of building burial chambers," said Gail.

Michael sighed. "You would think so. If there is a settlement, it's under the desert. Ann Lee led an effort to secure backing to fund an exploration, but unfortunately, we're short. As for the government, they're more interested in finding oil and minerals than artifacts. At least I came upon the infant mummy in my search. I was hoping we might get your university to help. Have you completed any tests yet?"

Nick motioned to the waiter to pour more wine. "We carbon dated the mummy at 3,798 years."

"We aren't sure about the cause of death," Gail added. "An MRI was run on it, but it didn't give us a cause of death."

Michael nodded enthusiastically. "Thank you for doing that. That's more than I hoped for. We may be on to something here. If Western settlements existed along this passageway into ancient China that long ago, then China could have been a world cultural center even at the time of the Xia dynasty. The Silk Road is thought to have been opened as the passageway to

China around 130 BC, but exchange between the East and the West could go back much further. Nick, can you set up a meeting for me with your department head?"

Gail looked at Nick with raised eyebrows.

"I think Gail would be the best one to do that. I had a kind of ...." He pushed a scallop around in circles in the melted butter.

"Falling out," Gail finished Nick's sentence and reached for his arm. "He was fired today because he tried to do things a little too fast. Butted heads with his boss."

"Oh no, that's terrible," Michael said. "I hope I'm not to blame."

Ann Lee looked at Michael. "*Weiji*. In crisis there is opportunity. This is the incipient moment."

"Did you burn the bridge?" Michael asked.

"To cinders."

"I may be able to help you. I read your work on desert excavation in Peru and it is noteworthy. I need your experience and ability, Nick. You would be a real asset for us. Of course, the pay is not as good as in America, but I should be able to offer you a good position with the Xinjiang Regional Museum as a field archaeologist project leader. I can have an offer of employment ready for you tomorrow. Think it over."

Nick slid his hand under the table and squeezed Gail's knee. "You can count on that, Michael. Would I be working out of the museum?"

Michael filled up their wine glasses. "Yes. And anywhere in Northwestern China, but initially in Shamadù." He held up his glass. "To the future."

"No. To the past," said Nick. They touched their glasses, and he took a deep swallow.

Gail pulled her business card from her purse and wrote Mohr's extension and email address on the back. "I'll try to arrange a meeting with John Mohr," she said, handing it to Michael. "He's the one to talk to, but there is also a university global fund that could help. I should know by tomorrow."

"I'll wait to hear from you," said Michael, smiling. "So, where is the menu?"

Over dessert, Michael talked of the rising incidence of looting and his fear that the ancient artifacts would be stolen and sold on the black market by the time they got there to discover them. "Some of the looters are better equipped than us. And smarter."

❧

After dinner Nick and Gail left in high spirits. Gail drove slowly back to her house. "Are you going to take the job?" she asked as they pulled into her driveway.

"How could I refuse? There's no place like Xinjiang. It's everything I always wanted to do." He put his hand on hers. "Something's holding me back."

"What's that?"

He looked into her eyes. "I would really miss you. I could probably find another job and not have to move."

She leaned toward him, and they kissed, tasting intimacy for the first time. "Come on in."

Nick followed her inside.

Gail turned on a small table lamp. It cast a warm glow over the room and left a few shadows for the imagination. The light played over carefully arranged Impressionist paintings and the abstract shapes of smooth African masks that hung on the walls.

"How about a glass of wine?" she asked. "I have dry or sweet."

"Bright with a lingering aftertaste of … something that tastes like you."

"I can do buttery."

She returned with two glasses and a bottle of red wine. After she poured, Nick touched his glass to hers. He raised it to his lips, more aware of the scent of her perfume than the bouquet of the wine.

Gail sat next to him on the couch. "Your future is looking bright. I knew you'd find something better."

"If I take the job, will you visit me?"

"If I can. That's a huge desert over there. You're going to need satellite imaging at some point. And an expert who knows how to do it." She tilted her head and grinned mischievously.

Nick smiled back wistfully and pointed to a copper mask on the wall. "Do you miss Africa?"

"I do. I spent two years on a dig in Nigeria. That's a copy of the Mask of Obulufon, who was a king and deity in ancient Ifé. When a new king took the throne, he would put it on and become the reincarnation of Obulufon. Like the stones on the Blue Baby's eyes, masks are gateways into other worlds."

Nick peered inside the emptiness of the mask through slits that had been cut out for once-living eyes. "It was so eerie looking at those stones. I felt like I was being transported through time."

"You're still here as far as I can tell."

He put down his glass. "It's time for me to get in my wreck and drive home. I enjoyed the evening."

Gail kissed him goodnight at the door. "Me too. Let me know what you decide."

After breakfast the next morning Nick got estimates to repair his car. It took half the day to find a body shop. While waiting for the keys to the loaner, he got a call from Gail.

"I was able to arrange a meeting with Mohr and Michael Chou, but he wasn't able to obtain support from the university. Mohr told Michael he would never get approval for the spending."

"I think Mohr could have been more open minded. He could get the money if he wanted to."

"It's not over by a long shot. Your friend is a regular Barnum and Bailey. He said he's going to *Discovery International Magazine* and *National Anthropology* to promote the finds you and he will make in Xinjiang. Then there will be money pouring in from all over the world. If the media gets in on it, they will come."

"Who am I, Indiana Jones?"

Gail laughed. "Think of what you can post on Facebook."

"Somebody get me a bullwhip."

$$\infty$$

Michael's decision to plant ideas in leading media channels was a long-range plan, but one that could bear fruit later. If he succeeded in gaining their ear, everything else would fall into place, including financial backing and international support.

An overnight letter on official museum letterhead arrived at Nick's house the following afternoon. After reading it carefully, he called Michael to discuss it. The work involved everything he had hoped for, and Michael explained that the salary may seem low, but it would let him live very well over there.

Nick accepted the offer. "When can I start?"

"You have made me very happy; you start right now. I will need to get you an alien travel permit, so you will be able to work in some restricted places. You'll need to apply for a six-month business visa and some other special work permits too. I will give you the addresses and phone numbers."

"Gail told me about your promotional plans. Should I bring my Indiana Jones hat?"

Michael laughed. "Better to dress like the locals. It's not Hollywood. In Urumqi, it won't matter. It's modern: lots of skyscrapers, all the conveniences. Outside the city are oasis towns and the desert."

"That's the Taklamakan, isn't it?"

"It means he who goes in does not come out, but you will do fine. After you are settled, I will need you to start your research on tombs in the area of Shamadù."

Other than uncertainty about subletting the house, everything clicked into place. Nick took care of his preparations in less than a week. Michael still needed a few extra days to sow his fundraising seeds and would catch up with him later.

"Go ahead without me, Nick. I'm going to do some networking and give a speech or two," Michael told him. "When you get there, look around and take time to find a nice place to live and see the sights. The Hetian Street Residential District would be an easy commute to the museum. When I get back, I'll take you through and introduce you to everyone."

Nick checked the flight schedules. It looked like a total flying time of about twenty-one hours, not including the flight to Los Angeles. He called Gail and told her of his plans, then asked her out to dinner on his last night before leaving. They decided on a Szechwan restaurant in Chinatown. When they were seated, he gave her a small box tied with a ribbon. Inside was an intricately wrought jade necklace.

"It's from the Qing dynasty, not very old, but I thought you might like it."

"I love it. Put it on for me."

Nick fastened the clasp for her, then kissed her neck.

They went back to Nick's house after dinner. He had

packed up his personal effects and put them in storage, leaving only the basic furnishings that would be rented with the house.

Gail put her arms around him. "Write me. Promise."

Nick closed his eyes and held her tightly. "Tomes. I won't forget."

In the morning she drove him to the airport, then walked with him to the gate at the departure terminal. They kissed goodbye, and soon she was waving through the window of the observation deck as the plane taxied down the runway.

Chapter Three:

The Land of Fruits and Melons

THE PLANE TOUCHED DOWN in Hong Kong at 4:10 am.
The last jaunt to Xinjiang was a six-hour stint. Much of the
flight to Urumqi passed over the Tien Shen, or Heavenly Mountains. When he looked out the window, the mountaintops
looked close, even from the high altitude of the jetliner. White
with snow and glaciers, often enclosed in thick cloud cover, the
mountains divided Xinjiang into northern and southern areas. Far to the northwest lay the tomb of Mongolian Emperor
Genghis Khan. On both sides of the mountains were mosques,
cave dwellings, and ancient ruins of Buddhist temples.

The mountains contained glaciers that fed lakes and riv-
ers. One glacier-fed river, the Tarim, flowed into a large river
basin called the Tarim Basin, which in turn, became part of
the Taklamakan Desert. Far to the south of the basin and the
Taklamakan, lay the small town of Shamadù at the foothills of

the Kunlun Mountains. Bordered by the Cherchen Desert and an ancient dried-up lakebed, it was an insalubrious place with extremes of temperature ranging from sub-zero to 106 degrees Fahrenheit. Storms occurred on the Cherchen Desert 145 days a year, sometimes with hurricane-force winds, causing the sand to penetrate and clog machinery. During the storms breathing, navigation, and travel are nearly impossible. Heavy winds blow almost every afternoon, making it advisable to stay indoors.

He would begin his search for Sorenson's mummies in Shamadù. Pulling out a small notebook, Nick made a list of things he would need to locate burial chambers and buried ruins: radio-carbon and potassium argon dating equipment, synthetic aperture radar equipment to detect objects under the sand, Mercedes-Benz Unimogs for desert travel, and global-positioning receivers for desert navigation. He would have to review the expertise available for a search team after he started at the museum. He added a bullet: Gail has friends at NASA. She might be able to aid in radar imaging.

In contrast to the hostile desert are the oasis towns on the old Silk Road, an ancient East-West trade route. Many were given their names by geographer Ferdinand von Richthofen. Often prosperous agricultural and trading centers, they give the region the Chinese nickname the Land of Fruits and Melons.

Nick landed at noon, China time. The official Chinese time system results in the sun rising at 8 am and setting at 11 pm in Urumqi. When Nick got off the plane it looked like mid-morning instead of lunchtime. The local Uyghur time was two hours ahead of official time, which seemed to make more sense, but Urumqi was 85 percent Han Chinese.

When he reached customs, the official spoke to him in Uyghur. Nick didn't understand, asking in Mandarin if the agent spoke English. "*Ni huì shuō yīngwén ma?*"

The round-eyed Uyghur official shook his head and searched Nick's luggage thoroughly, examining his papers and nodding to him to proceed.

Nick left customs and hailed a taxi. "*Yu Din,*" he told the driver.

Passing through the bustling downtown, he noticed the absence of American chain stores and smiled happily.

The taxi turned onto Xibei Road and, after a short ride, pulled into the courtyard of a large twelve-story hotel, the Yu Din. Nick paid the driver and checked into the room he had reserved the week before. It was spacious by Asian standards, with a TV and private bathroom.

Nick hung up his American pants and shirts, which were suitable enough for a modern city like Urumqi, but unfit for desert travel. Fall was approaching, a season of plunging temperatures and inhospitable weather. He decided to dress like the locals, and would need a hat, some woolen socks, and a pair of thick boots.

After lying on the bed for half an hour, Nick still couldn't fall asleep and took the elevator to the lobby. The concierge told him a street market was within walking distance. He strolled down Jiefang Nan Lu which opened onto the Erdao Qiao market, a traditional Uyghur covered market with vendors of many ethnicities, goods, and dishes. The sound of people speaking in different tongues created an otherworldly cacophony as each merchant extolled the virtues of their wares. Pakistani traders ran from stall to stall yelling and making deals. Carpet sellers hung brightly colored Heitan wool rugs and felt mats. Uyghur bootmakers, animal skin traders, and black-market moneychangers were at work. The air was rich with the scent of cumin, coriander, sweet clove, caraway, fennel, and even Queen Anne's lace.

Nick spotted an elderly milliner sitting at an old sewing machine powered by a foot pedal. A twelve-year-old boy, probably his grandson, stacked the hats he had made on a table nearby. Nick found a flat cap that was popular with the locals and tried it on.

"*Es salaam aleikum,*" the man said to Nick.

"*Wa aleikum es salaam,*" he replied in the little Uyghur he knew. He tapped the hat. "How much?"

"*Oute yuan,*" the man replied, feeding more cloth under the needle.

"Five yuan," the boy translated.

"That's fine. I'll take it. It will be a good hat to wear in the desert."

The boy translated back to the milliner.

The old man snatched the hat from Nick's head. He

yanked on it, tearing apart the seams in one great pull, speaking quickly in Uyghur all the while.

Startled, Nick assumed the man didn't like Americans.

"*Yakshee emess*, you wait, mister, no good. He fix hat for you," the boy said.

The milliner cut an extra piece of lining material from a bolt of cloth and sewed it into the hat, using double the amount of stitching this time. The boy again translated. "He say you need thick hat to go to that place. He made it for desert, no extra charge."

"What do I owe?" Nick asked.

The milliner shook his head. The boy said, "No more, mister."

Nick was touched by his kindness. "Tell him thank you."

"*Rachmet*," the boy said to his grandfather.

The old man broke into a smile. Smiling back, Nick put on his new hat.

Hungry from the many aromas mingling in the air, he decided trying Uyghur food. One vendor served a dish called *laghman* that was made with mutton, fresh eggplant, string beans, tomatoes, and hot peppers on a bed of noodles. Other dishes consisted of kebabs and nan. Manta, a thin-skinned dumpling filled with mutton and onion, looked appealing. One stall in particular fascinated Nick. In it was a large cauldron containing a soup called *apke*. Simmering in a broth of entrails, a goat's head rested atop a coil of intestines that had been cleaned and stuffed with meat, flour, eggs, and oil. *If you are going to live here*, his inner dialogue argued, *you have to keep an open mind*. All the same, he decided on *laghman* and chai.

For dessert he ate a *durap*, a dish made from yogurt, honey, and chipped ice, then headed back to his hotel room. It was still light, so he closed the curtains, undressed, and climbed into bed.

℘

When he awoke ten hours later, he felt alert and ready for the day. After shaving and dressing he returned to the marketplace to eat. He wolfed down a *samsa*, a bun made with lamb fat and onion, then walked to Xinhua Lu Street where he hailed a taxi to take him to Xinjiang Auto Rental.

The driver deposited Nick in a large lot filled with BYDs, Toyotas, and Land Rovers. After looking over several vehicles he decided to rent a Land Rover with a stick shift and air conditioning.

Nick asked the rental agent for directions to the museum. Taking Xi Bei Lu, he arrived at the museum complex a few minutes later. The Xinjiang Regional Museum was a modern stone block building with twelve arched windows and a two-story arc-shaped entrance. A dome rose in the center of the structure. The large wings on both sides of the building balanced the strong center portion, promising to hold many great exhibits within.

As he walked through the giant entrance doors, the presence of the past enveloped him. The museum spoke a language of its own, and Nick felt at home.

Two hours passed, and it was time to start looking for a place to live. On his way out, he picked up a postcard with a photo of the museum for Gail. A newspaper stand outside the museum carried a renter's guide. He picked one up and located some high-rise apartments in the Hetian Street Residential District Michael had recommended, an easy commute to the museum. After an afternoon of apartment hunting, he found one that looked promising.

His first impression of the exotic marketplace and the Heavenly Mountains had flamed his passion for exploration. He became impatient to see the oasis towns and scout out locations for digs. A stop at a map shop yielded good maps of Xinjiang and the oasis towns along the Silk Road.

It was early evening when Nick returned to his hotel room. He called room service, ordered dinner, and then sat down to write Gail about the sights he had seen. After the food arrived, he spread out a map of the region on his desk, weighting the corners down with salt and pepper shakers.

Shamadù was far to the south, at least 640 miles of difficult driving. Michael had told him that there was a legend of an older city buried under the desert somewhere in that vicinity, but no trace had ever been found. Archaeologists referred to it as the Lost City of Old Shamadù. Research had indicated there had been more water there three thousand years ago, and that the old city might have been far more prosperous and strategically important than the present-day town.

The ruins of Jiaohe and the Bezeklik Thousand Buddha Caves in Turpan were only about ninety miles away from Urumqi, and he had just one more day before starting work. Early the next morning, he handed the hotel clerk the museum postcard and the letter to Gail to mail and left the Yu Din. After tanking up the Rover and throwing an extra can of water in the back, he was satisfied with his preparations for the trip to Turpan.

Leaving the congestion of the city behind, he drove an hour and a half to Jiaohe, an ancient city hewn from mud dating back to 300 BC. Many dwellings, now ruins, were below ground and lined with brick. Nick spent a lot of time at the Cheshi Museum. The Cheshi were an ethnic group of Caucasians who had settled in the area and built the City of Jiaohe which once held over 7,000 people. Libraries of documents written in Tocharian had been left behind in the first millennium, but it was uncertain if the Tocharians were descended from the Cheshi.

Nick's next stop was the Thousand Buddhist Caves at Bezeklik, Turpan. There were far too many to take in on one trip, but he made it a point to stop in at Cave 31, an eleventh century cave painted during Uyghur rule that had been recommended by a tour guide at Jiaohe. In one painting, a group of male musicians of various cultures played together with a drum and different wind instruments. The musicians appeared to be

Uyghurs, a dark-skinned South Asian man, and a Caucasian. It was an indication that the society living there at that time was a melting pot of races.

When he arrived back at the hotel in the evening, a telegram from Michael Chou was waiting. Michael was back and would pick him up at the Yu Din at nine in the morning.

☙

"How did it go in the States? Did you find some backers?" asked Nick as he got in the car.

Michael shrugged. "It went well enough. We didn't get any promises, but we got their ear. When we find the tomb, they will probably do a special. I'm going to be meeting with CCTV and the BBC to see if they want to get in on it, too."

Michael drove Nick to look at a furnished apartment for rent at the corner of Hetian Street and Wuyi Road, only a few blocks from the Chou's condominium. It was the one that Nick had liked the day before. The landlord recognized Nick and shook his hand. "We saved it for you," he said with a smile.

"Good view of the expressway," said Michael, looking out the window.

"It's only fifteen minutes to the museum from here. G216 takes you most of the way," the landlord replied nervously.

Nick tried the burners on the stove. "Nice and clean. Does it have Wi-Fi?"

"Oh yes. Very fast."

Michael leaned on the kitchen table, and it rocked unevenly. "Is the floor uneven?"

"I'll have the legs tightened," said the landlord. He came down on the price and Nick agreed to take it. All Nick needed to do was bring his luggage in the evening.

"It's a nice apartment. I think you got a good deal," said Michael as they returned to the car.

Nick laughed. "I appreciate your help. I think you had him squirming a little."

"Don't think anything of it." Michael turned onto the entrance ramp of G216. "By the way, you need to register your cell phone with the police. It's something new they require of foreigners. You should do it in the next day or two, after you get settled in."

"I haven't turned on my cell phone since I got here; it's too expensive to use an American phone. I thought I'd just get a new one here or change the chip. What's the idea; squash foreign competition? What happens if I don't register it?"

Michael accelerated into an open spot in the fast lane. "It's complicated. In Xinjiang, they are afraid terrorists use social media, so the Chinese government has forbidden everyone to use Facebook, Twitter, or YouTube, and has blocked them with this thing called the Great Firewall. The only way to get through the Great Firewall is to turn on VPN, and that is forbidden. They require every phone to have a proper ID and VPN hides the ID. So now all Uyghurs, and foreigners, must register with the police or their phones will be turned off. New phones or not."

"I use VPN to connect to my bank online."

"Not a good idea, my friend. There is a China Telecom near your apartment on Yutian Street. They'll get you fixed up, then you better visit the police. I know … pain in the butt."

They drove to the museum parking lot to an open space near the courtyard marked DIRECTOR. "I'll show you your office and introduce you to the staff," said Michael as they approached the new structure. "I liked the old building a little better; it was sort of Russian and Uyghur melded together. It felt more exotic, more like Xinjiang, somehow."

"I went through just to get a feel for things when I first got here," said Nick. "The inside still has that museum feel. I'll be right at home. But I know what you mean. I'm surprised how modern the new one is."

They walked by the visitor desk as they entered. "Hello, Mr. Chou," said a college girl at the desk. Michael returned her greeting with a smile.

"We have interns from Xinjiang University working here," he explained. "The university is practically next door. They have a good archaeology department. One of the reasons the government tore down the old museum and built this was to promote ethnic unity in Xinjiang. We have exhibits representing the twelve ethnic groups in Xinjiang. In Urumqi, there are mostly Han Chinese, in the south of Xinjiang there are mostly

Uyghur, and there is also a mix of Kazaks and Uzbeks, Tatars, Pamiris, Hui, and Mongol, and some Russian, and others. We include all peoples, and mummies of all kinds. The mummies have their own wing."

They came to doors at the end of the hall with a sign reading MUSEUM STAFF ONLY. Michael pressed his finger on the door sensor and they opened. "This is our staff wing. The living have it good, too."

Michael led Nick to a room filled with live screen images of the exhibits and valuable artifacts on display. He introduced him to the security director, Lu Wang, and his assistant, Alim Azmat. Nick had his picture taken for his employee ID.

After Nick pinned on his badge, he was taken to meet Dr. Zhang Xue, head of the archaeology department. "You two will be working together on the Shamadù Project," said Michael.

Xue bowed his head and Nick returned the formality. "I am pleased you have decided to join us. I understand you have spent several years at Chan Chan in Chimor, Peru. We need your desert skills," said the archaeologist.

"I read your book on the excavations in Loulan, Doctor. I still have a lot to learn."

"The Taklimakan has some unique surprises. It may take some getting used to."

"The sooner I get started the better," said Nick.

Xue smiled. "I'm looking forward to working with you."

Michael guided Nick into the hall. "I'm going to show

Nick around some more. He'll have the office across the hall, so you'll be able to get together later."

By the time they had visited all the museum staff, Nick was sure he couldn't remember another name. In the early afternoon, they took a break and left to have lunch at a café down the street.

"When we find the mummies in Shamadù, how will you fit them in with the others? The wing is crowded already," said Nick, as they sat at a table.

"I'm still thinking about it." Michael took a bite from a pork belly bun. "Maybe we will need a temporary display down in Shamadù to get things started while we bring in the media. We can set up tents or yurts to protect them until we can come up with something permanent in the museum. Who knows, we might send them on a world tour as the mummy wing is expanded."

Chapter Four:

Barnum and Bailey

THE NEXT MORNING MICHAEL called Nick and Xue into his office and motioned to them to take a seat. "There are paradigm shifts underway in Xinjiang," said Michael. We have to think fifty years from now. The oasis towns in Shamadù will no longer be isolated outposts. Tourists will arrive there in bus loads on new highways to visit the ruins and tombs, and it won't all be tourists, either. The desert will be irrigated with glacial runoff and agriculture and industry will return to the region. Plans for population movement, hospitals, airports, and schools are in motion as we speak."

Xue leaned forward in his seat. "We must identify areas of archaeological importance and educate builders and construction crews on identifying relics and ancient sites. Farmers, too. Things are turning up in the fields in the mainland all the time. It'll be the same in Xinjiang."

"Absolutely," Michael said. "We must begin planning now. I have been in communication with the Xinjiang and Chinese archeological societies, and we will be working with them to develop education programs. Unfortunately, the central government has a history of disinterest when it involves spending money on anything other than commercial development. They have traditionally thought of Xinjiang as the place of barbarians. Other than our museum here, I am not expecting much financial support. That is why I have been campaigning for funds in America. As P. T. Barnum said, 'Without promotion, something terrible happens... nothing.'"

"So, we have to give them a show," said Nick.

Michael smiled wryly. "A three-ring circus."

"Why am I not thrilled?"

"Come on. You speak English better than any of us and you are an excellent public speaker. Plus, you have lots of team leadership experience."

"I'm an even better field archeologist," said Nick.

"Don't you worry. You're going to have blisters and feel sore all over."

Nick beamed. "That sounds more like it."

"What is the plan?" asked Xue.

"I want the two of you to establish a camp near Charbashi, where we found the Blue Baby," said Michael. "Sorenson's tomb must be somewhere in that vicinity. I want you two to walk the land and get the coordinates for the satellite imaging to me. I'll get permission from the government to do the scans. Once we have located and unearthed the tomb, catalogue and photograph everything. Then we call in the press and tell the world. It will be the greatest show on earth. Everybody will want to get into the act."

"Even John Mohr," said Nick. "You are brilliant."

Xue looked up from the notes he was taking. "We'll need a crew. At least four."

"That's true," said Michael, "but we are broke. You two are the only crew for now. I'll take care of the permits and put together the equipment for you. While that is in progress, do some preliminary research on the origins of the mummies here in Xinjiang. We need to emphasize how little we know, and how much research remains to be done. I'll use it in an information package to attract donors."

"I'll show Nick how to access the university library," said Xue.

"Good. You and Nick get started on it. We have to work fast, the cold weather will be here soon. You should be on your way to Shamadù by the middle of next week."

❧

A few days later the Land Rover sat in the museum parking lot, loaded and ready. Michael came out to see Xue and Nick off. "Call me with a progress report at the end of each day, Nick."

Nick shook his head. "I still don't have approval for a phone yet. The police said it may take another week."

"It just keeps getting worse. Okay, Xue. You check in."

They left the congestion of the city behind and drove an hour and a half to an area of green fields and soda-whitened marshes outside the town of Karashahr, or Black Town. Xue directed Nick to turn onto a road which led to several ancient ruins and the rammed earth walls of an abandoned city dating back to the Han dynasty.

"I'll need to get some photos," Xue said. "Let me out by those mounds."

They stopped by a path leading to the mounds. "I would love to excavate those," Nick said. At one time Karashahr held a largely Indo-European, Tocharian-speaking population like Jiaohe. He wondered if the mounds held any clues about the people who once lived there and the long dead Tocharian language.

After Xue got the photos he needed, they continued through the northern wastes of the Taklamakan and passed through the Iron Gate Pass, the historic military bottleneck and stronghold that protected the southern region of the Silk Road from northern invaders. Further on they came to the town of Korla, and found a place to stay the night at the Bayinguoleng Binguan. It wasn't as luxurious as the Yu Din, but was clean and comfortable.

An attendant carrying a thermos let them into their room. "Where do people go to eat?" Nick asked.

The attendant poured out a glass of boiled water. "The Bodun. Very good food, reasonable prices, but no alcohol. It's down the street."

Thanking the attendant, he and Xue walked two blocks to the restaurant. Once inside, they were directed to a table. When the waiter asked Nick what he would like for dinner, Nick pointed to a lamb dish nearby that looked good. A musician began playing a dotar and a dancer twirled about the table, adding to the enjoyment of the meal.

After diner, they returned to the hotel, which overlooked the edge of the city and out over the desert. The horizon was a serene unobstructed spectacle. The stars stood out in the cold night sky like sparkling jewels. At that moment, it was hard to believe the Taklamakan was one of the harshest deserts in the world.

In the morning, they were awakened by the muezzin's call to prayer from the minaret of a nearby mosque. After a light breakfast, they began the longest stretch of road on the trip.

The Tarim Highway began at Korla and spanned all the way across the desert to the town of Niya. It was built to transport the oil and minerals found in the Taklamakan. Although not filled with archeological ruins like the roads on the circumference of the desert, the Tarim Highway was a much faster route to Shamadù.

Out on the highway the only traffic was an occasional

truck or oil tanker. Rows of reed fences had been erected to slow down the flow of sand dunes, but even with these measures sand still drifted on the road surface and had to be shoveled off by road workers at intervals along the way.

The desert dunes were only a few feet high and looked more like a seascape than a landscape. In ancient times travelers would take months to travel to Italy, Greece, India or Persia on the Silk Road, crossing the desert at night using camels to carry five hundred pound loads. After the Silk Road was first established, travelers would hear whispering voices from the desert which led them off the road. They would lose their sense of direction and become lost, never to be seen again.

Travelers died from the harsh conditions of the Taklamakan, even into the beginning of the twentieth century. The trip used to take three weeks, but Nick and Xue would make it in three days in the air-conditioned comfort of their Land Rover. Michael had predicted that within less than a decade, legions of tourists would travel through by bus to visit the new discoveries they were about to make.

The dunes passed by for hours in hypnotic progression. The dancer and the stars of the desert he had witnessed the night before floated through his mind in a daydream as the air over the roadway ahead became translucent with haze.

"Be careful," said Xue. "Looks like a sand storm."

Nick slowed down and continued for several miles, trying to squint through the murk. A thick curtain of reddish cloud suddenly enveloped them, blanketing the highway. As they entered the blast, the tires hit a wave of sand on the road, sending the Rover into the air. It hit the ground on two wheels and skidded sideways. Nick had enough presence of mind to steer with the slide, as though he were driving in snow. The vehicle stabilized and emerged into bright sunlight as though there never had been a storm.

They drove on without further incident to Niya. The town, which was on the original southern Silk Road, had been colonized by ancient Indians from an area of today's Pakistan known then as Taxila. The Hungarian-British archaeologist, Aural Stein, had unearthed orchards and gardens in Niya from sixteen centuries ago, indicating that both Niya and Shamadù had more water in ancient times.

As the water supply decreased, Niya's prosperity declined into the early twentieth century. When it came under the rule of the People's Republic of China after the Second World War, its standard of living was improved. Better irrigation systems were introduced, a school was built, and telephones were installed in many households. When the Tarim Highway was completed, Niya's location at the intersection of two key roads made it more important. A department store was built on the main street.

Nick found a café to relax in after the long drive. A Chinese man followed them into the café. "Are you English?" he asked Nick.

"American," Nick answered.

He took a seat next to Nick. "That is great; I'll still get a chance to use my English. My name is Jih-Wen Chang. Are you here on business, may I ask?"

"I'm Nick Taylor. This is Zhang Xue. We're with the Xinjiang Regional Museum, doing some archaeological scouting." Nick stuck out his hand.

"You will need people who know the desert," said Chang, shaking Nick's hand. "I know some guides if you need them. Diggers, too."

"We may take you up on that. We'll be organizing searches in Shamadù. I'm hoping we can locate some buried tombs and buildings. Do you know of any ruins around here?"

"No, I don't. I've heard of The Lost City of Shamadù, but no one has ever found it. There are the ruins of a temple called Charbashi you may find interesting. It's about six miles north of Shamadù, out in the desert."

"That's where we're heading," said Xue."

"You better watch out. It's a bad stretch of road as you travel eastward. There were heavy winds a few days ago. It may still be covered by sand in places. Even without the sand it's winding and hard to follow. When you get to Shamadù you will find it is a poor town. There has been less water from the mountains each year; the people can't grow enough to eat anymore."

Chang told them of a guesthouse in Niya where they could spend the night, then said goodbye. Nick and Xue ate a light dinner at the café, then made their way to the guesthouse.

"Seemed like a nice fellow," said Nick, getting out of the Rover and stretching. "Maybe we can use him."

"He seems too needy to me," said Xue.

"I don't know what you mean."

Xue pulled his pack out of the back. "Too friendly. He wants something."

"Sure, a job."

"Maybe I'm wrong."

The next morning, the wind was blowing hard enough to kick up a haze of dust and it had gotten colder. They tanked up the Rover and headed out to the highway. The dunes were over three hundred feet high, steep, and crescent-shaped. To the right, the snow-capped Kunlun rose into the air. They contained glaciers that feed the Cherchen River, which works its way northward through the desert past the town of Shamadù and disappears in the sand.

Travel along this road was much slower than on the Tarim Highway. It broke into rocky patches in places and in others was covered by sand. Occasionally storm-squalls mixed flakes of snow into the dusty haze, making visibility worse. The dust found its way through the air circulation system of the Land Rover and coated everything inside in a thick layer. Outside it stuck to the windshield and body, turning the vehicle from cream to beige. They finally pulled into Shamadù in the early afternoon, coated and tired from the difficult driving.

Jih-Wen Chang's description of the town was accurate. The main street was lined with low wattle and daub houses. Stepping out of the Rover, the weary travelers were greeted by a cold, sand-saturated wind that stung their faces and eyes. They pushed their way through the grit storm to a café that was as empty as the street. A disheveled waiter with red-rimmed eyes appeared through a curtain from a room in the back.

They each ordered a coffee, then Nick explained what he was looking for in Mandarin. When it was evident the waiter didn't understand, Xue repeated it in Uyghur. The waiter shook his head and said he knew of no artifacts or tombs and turned to get their coffee.

"We need to find a place to spend the night," Nick said.

Xue spun around in his seat to ask, but the waiter had already parted the curtains, revealing an old man toking on a hookah. The waiter spoke rapidly to the man, who nodded as he refrained from answering in order to hold in a lungful of hashish smoke.

"Those guys are a bunch of stoners," said Nick.

Xue laughed. "No wonder the waiter's eyes are so red. Well, we are in Xinjiang."

Nick sipped his coffee slowly, wondering if the wind would die down long enough for them to do a little exploring before heading to the Charbashi ruins in the morning to set up their camp. No matter what, he was getting a feel for what he was up against. Just as they were about to leave, the waiter returned with the old man.

The man spoke in Mandarin in a raspy voice. "I am told you are looking for something in the desert."

Nick stood and offered his hand, but it was not taken. "Yes. We are archaeologists from the museum in Urumqi. We're looking for relics. Old objects like statues and bowls, or a brass pot or jar. Especially from the desert. I'm looking for stories, too. About temples, ruins. Legends about tombs buried out there in the desert."

His brows knitted. "There is a ruin of an old Buddhist monastery about five miles from here. It has been eaten away by the wind and sand. A few miles past a mummy was found."

"Which direction was that?"

He pointed a bony finger over Nick's shoulder.

"Can you take me there?"

"My son knows where, you will need to ask him."

"Where can I find him?" asked Nick.

"He is working at the oil fields. He will be coming home in a few days."

"Is there some way we could get out there today? Perhaps someone would go with us in the Land Rover?"

"You must go on foot or camel. Your Land Rover will sink in the sand. There is a storm coming; it is better to stay in town." He put his hand firmly on Nick's shoulder. "Wait a few days. It would be better if my son took you, he knows the desert very well.”

“I see,” said Nick. “Thank you for all your help.”

Xue pointed to the hookah just behind the curtains. “Have you ever tried it?”

“What? Hashish?” asked Nick.

“These storms can last for days and there is nothing to do, believe me. It helps you relax. I’m going to smoke. You are welcome to join me. The good stuff comes from Xinjiang, right around here.”

Nick’s jaw dropped. “But it’s illegal.”

Xue smiled angelically. “In Urumqi you go to jail. Here, no one cares. It’s an old tradition.”

Half an hour later, Nick and Xue climbed into the Rover and ambled slowly up the street to a dormitory style guesthouse. They had the place to themselves and spread out a map of the desert on an empty bed. The map covered a huge area of 143,000 square miles. The distance from the town of Shamadù to where Michael had found the Blue Baby appeared as a small puddle jump on the map.

Nick went to the window and looked out over the desert. The wind was still blowing as night fell and visibility was poor. A gust of wind pelted sand against the glass and Nick laughed out loud.

“What’s so funny?” said Xue.

"In English we say, 'it's raining cats and dogs.' What do you say?"

Xue thought for a moment. "I am Cantonese. We say," Xue struggled to keep a straight face, then burst out laughing, "… we say: 'dog poo is falling.'"

Nick rolled on the floor. "My God, that makes no sense at all."

"Don't tell me I make no sense, when you are telling me it rains cats and dogs."

Nick got on his hands and knees. "Okay, but this makes sense."

"What?"

"The French say, 'it's raining like a pissing cow.'"

Xue grabbed his stomach. "Ha, ha, ha. I like that."

After they could laugh no longer, Nick gave Xue a bag of trail nuts and lay on his bed. He opened Sir Aurel Stein's *Ancient Khotan*, eating from his last bag of nuts as he read. A bare bulb overhead produced just enough light by which to read. The walls of the guesthouse were thick, but the mournful shrieking of the wind still penetrated through them. His rib ached from the laughter, but it was dulled from the hashish. He pushed the pain to the back of his mind with the aid of the book. A few chapters later he crawled under the thin blanket and fell asleep fully clothed.

"Nicholas." He awoke with a start, not sure someone called his name or if he was dreaming. Xue was sound asleep, snoring on his bed on the other side of the room. Something was different. The wind had stopped and a still silence permeated the room. His watch said three am. His rib was throbbing and he couldn't go back to sleep. Nick put on his Uyghur cap and wool coat and went outside. The full moon shone through the cold air, lighting up the nightscape. He walked to the back of the building and looked in the direction the old man had indicated the ruin lay. Between the open spaces of the dunes he could see with his binoculars the time-sculpted outline of Charbashi rising above the desert floor. One corner of the building had crumbled away, cloaked in shadow. "Nicholas," said the voice.

He turned in a slow circle, searching for the source, but no one was there. There weren't any signs of the storm the old man talked about. He thought he could make it out to the ruins before dawn, look around a bit, and be back in time for a late breakfast. After all, the caravans traveled at night.

Ignoring the warning, he ran back inside and wrote a note to Xue, then grabbed a canteen and flashlight and started out across the desert in the bright moonlight. He sighted the North Star and noted its position in relation to the ruins. The temperature had dropped below freezing, making the air brisk and invigorating.

The softness of the sand absorbed the forward momentum of walking, but overall progress was good. The moon shadows lengthened as he approached the ruins. He was another half hour away when the shadows suddenly disappeared. Ragged clouds obscured the moon for several minutes, then the bright glow commenced again. Nick maintained his sense of direction and continued. A few minutes later the moon was blanketed again. Heavy clouds poured through the skies and darkened the landscape. Sand began to rise from the desert floor, making a soft sighing sound as the rising wind blew through it.

"Nicholas," the voice whispered.

Startled, he turned around to locate the source, but once more, no one was there. Looking up to check his orientation, the North Star had disappeared, obscured by the dust and clouds. He couldn't see the town or the ruins either. Nick remembered a hundred-foot high dune on his right.

He pulled out his flashlight, lighting up the dune. As he swung it along the side and out into the open where he thought the ruins would lie, he saw the beam disappear into a thick suspension of air-borne sand. He walked around the dune and was hit by the full blast of the gale that now swept across the desert. The intense wind drove sand into his eyes and down his coat. His new hat went spinning into the night. Recoiling from the blast, he stepped back behind the safety of the dune, unable to see, realizing how foolish he had been.

After several minutes of painful tearing his vision started to come back. Nick kicked himself for forgetting goggles; all he had was a pair of sunglasses in his coat pocket. Sand whorls danced about him; sand streamed over the top of the dune in driving sheets; sand poured into the crescent-shaped scoop on the backside. The ruins could provide refuge where he might be able to wait the storm out. They were only a half-mile more.

The sand continued to fill the air, getting in his eyes and finding its way down inside his clothing. He put on the sunglasses and held them on his head with one hand. The beam from the flashlight barely penetrated more than a few feet in front of him.

Screwing up his courage, he moved out from behind the dune, pushing his way against the wind, exposing himself to the full force of the gale that was still gaining velocity. He walked a hundred yards and had to stop. The sand was getting into his lungs.

He turned around 180 degrees and walked backward, pulling the coat collar over his mouth to breathe. After a few minutes, he had to close his eyes from the pain caused by the grit, then was forced to his knees. Nick was spent, panting in shallow breaths, feeling a strong desire to sleep.

Keep moving, get to the ruins, he told himself, walking like an automaton in reverse. He pushed backward through the blast, missing the ruins by a few hundred feet, too numb and blind to notice. He forced himself to keep going, realizing that was his key to survival.

Through the fog of his exhaustion, Nick had an odd sensation of sinking. There was some sort of depression in the sand and his feet were sliding down the sides as he moved them mechanically back and forth.

He stopped for a moment, and although he couldn't see, he

knew he was sinking. Sand poured into the depression around him, weighing against his legs, holding them still.

The din of the storm continued while the floor of the desert swallowed him up to his waist, then chest, and then over his shoulders. As the sand converged about his neck and reached his chin, he took what he thought was his last breath. Then the ground opened beneath him and he plunged downward through open space. It reminded him of a recurring nightmare he used to have as a child. He would fall into a sinkhole in the backyard. The dirt would give way and he would fall for what seemed an eternity. In his dream, he believed if he struck the bottom he would die and he would force himself awake to escape from the nightmare. At the last possible moment, he would waken, terrified.

Something tore at his side on the way down. He crashed down on a hard floor, knocking the wind out of him. In total silence and darkness, he gasped for air, down in a chamber under the desert.

Chapter Five:

Sorcerer

Nick regained his senses in blackness and freezing cold, but there was no wind. The quiet was complete and encompassing. It felt like the marrow of his bones had been sucked out and he was not sure whether he was dreaming or awake. Something sticky was on his side that felt like blood and his head was splitting.

Fumbling for the flashlight, he let the sand tear from his eyes. He found the switch and ran the beam along the floor, his mind reeling. He had landed in a long, narrow, mud-brick lined chamber with a ceiling made of smooth log beams supporting a coarse felt padding that served as a roof and supported the desert floor above. Shorter, thicker logs spanned the walls below the lengthwise beams, bearing the weight of the long ones, except where he lay. Several of the long beams had come loose and pivoted downward to the level of his head, only a foot off the floor. Sand had flowed down the incline of these fallen beams, sealing the chamber from the outside as it had been for millenniums. Along the length of the floor ran a drainage channel about two feet wide and a foot deep. Two plain wooden boxes, each the size of a person, lay along the sides of the chamber. A similar third box had been placed at the far end.

Satisfied there wasn't an immediate danger, he stood up cautiously and shook off the sand from his hair and clothes, then directed the beam into the far wooden box. In the lidless ancient coffin, he could see the mummified remains of a young woman. Some decomposition had occurred to the upper torso and face. A head strap had been placed under her chin to hold the jaws shut in death, but it had slipped off, allowing the swelling of the tongue to force her mouth open in a gruesome mummy gape. Nick moved the flashlight's beam over to the box along the side wall. Inside was another woman, almost six feet in length and dressed in a long fur cape with an elegant collar. She was remarkably preserved, with fair white skin and long auburn hair. Intricate tattoos adorned her face and hands. Colored woolen earrings hung from her earlobes. Her features were clearly Caucasoid.

Nick flinched, feeling blood trickling down his side. He turned the beam of light to the last box and looked in to discover a very tall man, at least six foot six and showing no signs of decomposition. He wore a dark maroon waistcoat and matching leggings. Brightly colored shanks of woolen material overhung the tops of deerskin boots. On his face were thin and intricate tattoos. It seemed impossible; here lay the tall man he had dreamed about.

The events of the last few weeks flashed through Nick's mind in a blur; his head started buzzing. The tattoos on the dead man's face drew his mind into their patterns and grew larger and more intricate, then changed shape, pulling Nick deeper into their maze. They were winding and unwinding at the same time, leading farther down into an underlying matrix of symbols and shapes that seemed to have a meaning or relevance that would flash into illumination just around the next fold, the next curve, the next cross point, always pulling him farther down. The buzzing grew louder and began echoing; a paralysis locked Nick into a trance. The whorl of the tattoo matrix continued its pull. He fell backwards, descending into another world.

Like falling down the sinkhole, he descended in a roller coaster plunge that wouldn't let go of his stomach. He expected to hit the bottom momentarily, but a flash of light exploded about him and surrounded him in a brilliant haze. Suddenly the tall man stood before him, holding out his hand. In it was a small flat bone with a hole, like in his dream.

"What are you?" asked Nick.

"We are one and the same," he replied.

"I don't know what you mean."

"One and the same, just in different sheaths. I am Tok Ma, you are Tok Ma."

"Sheaths?"

"You and I share the same soul, but there can only be one covering at a time. The answers are on the other side."

He held the bone in front of Nick's eyes.

"Look through the hole and enter."

On the other side of the opening was absolute nothingness; neither dark, light, up, down nor sideways, an infinity of possibilities that was not any one thing, but everything. In this void of existence was a chaotic miracle of expanding energy where shapes began to form, congealing and sharpening into striking clarity.

He found himself standing on the shore of a sparkling lake surrounded by green fields which commingled with desert in the distance. A waterfall cascaded down the rocky heights of the towering Kunlun Mountains to form the Shamadù River flowing through the desert into the lake.

In its still waters he saw his reflection; a tall man wearing a pointed narrow brimmed hat that dipped forward at the top, making him look like a sorcerer.

"I'm glad you're here, Tok Ma. Where have you been?" crackled an elderly voice from behind.

"I'm Nick Taylor," said Nick. He spun about on the heels of his deerskin boots.

"How strange. And I'm the Emperor of Xia. Let's go, the council is about to begin."

The old man seemed familiar. Nick stared intently, trying to recall where they met before.

"Why are you staring at me, Tok Ma? It's time to go."

"No, this isn't happening. My head hurts. Awfully bad."

"What has happened to you, are you under a spell? Can't you remember who you are, or for that matter, who I am?"

Nick dropped to his knees and held his head in his hands. He shut his eyes, rocking from side to side, trying to remember. There was the storm, the tomb, the hole in the bone.

"I looked through the hole in the bone."

The old man pressed his hands to Nick's forehead and Nick began to shake. He muttered an incantation and rubbed Nick's temples. Nick began to shake so fast he became a blur. "Stay with me. You are Tok Ma, what is my name?"

"Gon Ea? It comes back now. You are my teacher, Gon Ea."

"Once I looked through the bone myself, but never had the courage to pass through. You are a great wizard, Tok Ma. Tell me about the other side. What was there?"

Tok Ma put the bone in a pouch hanging from his side. "Another world, far in the future, so different from ours. The earth was filled with people everywhere, and incredible machines - they had so much learning, yet didn't know who they were. I was a scientist...."

"A scientist! What is that?" asked Gon Ea. "When we have the time, you must tell me more."

"Of course. Thank you for the wisdom you have bestowed, teacher. I would be an ignorant lump if not for you."

They walked along the shoreline until the earthen walls of ancient Shamadù revealed themselves. The town nestled in a valley that formed the basin for the lake, overlooked by a great wooden palace at the base of the mountains. Horses grazed in the surrounding gentle hills.

The two sorcerers proceeded through massive brass gates to a crowd of people assembled in the town square. The town elders stood beneath a large awning erected in the center to shield them from the sun.

A burly merchant dressed in a green plaid twill coat and trousers and wearing a beret with a peacock feather stood on a wooden box, speaking to the crowd angrily.

"Xie Pu has gone too far this time. We have been loyal servants to the emperors from time immemorial, but this one is not like his ancestors. He has taxed us into poverty and stolen our horses. He has made us slaves, but now he takes our daughters, too. We cannot endure it any longer."

Gon Ea prodded his companion. "Say something."

Nick looked helplessly about him, trying to focus. "Am I dreaming? Why should I say something?"

The old wizard eyed him sternly. "You are Tok Ma. You always know what to say. The people respect you."

Nick held his hands before his eyes, fascinated with the tattoos covering them. Looking at his hands brought his mind back into focus. He was Tok Ma.

An elder pointed to the wizard. "Look, Tok Ma is here."

"Speak, Tok Ma," chanted the crowd, pushing him through to the tent.

"What should we do, Tok Ma?" asked the elder.

Tok Ma looked at the faces in the crowd, sun beaten and creased, feeling their pain and anger. "Xie Pu is old. We have only to endure a while longer."

"Most of you are still too young to remember how we got here," said Gon Ea. We live only at the whim of the royal family. Lord Xie Pu is Emperor Jie's nephew; they could crush us any time they chose."

"Things are getting worse every day. We cannot continue like this," said the merchant. The crowd shouted approval.

"Be patient, friends," replied Tok Ma. "We must be calm and avoid bloodshed."

Encouraged by the crowd, the merchant shook his finger at the wizard. "Where have you been? Everyday more disappear without a trace. What's going on, Tok Ma? We need answers."

Tok Ma raised his arms in supplication, trying to maintain order. "I'll go to the mountains and find Fenghuang. The simurgh will know."

"We have never seen such a creature," someone yelled. "We need a warrior, not fairy tales."

A woman pushed her way through the crowd and stood by Tok Ma.

"Listen to my husband, don't be foolish. Give him three days to find the miraculous bird. Then we will know what to do."

The elders spoke among themselves; the chief raised his hands.

"Go, Tok Ma, find the simurgh and seek its counsel. We will meet here again in three days to hear what you have learned."

When the crowd had gone, Tok Ma took her in his arms and kissed her. "I missed you."

She pushed him away, smiling quizzically. "What has gotten in to you, husband?"

"It seems like forever."

She eyed him suspiciously. "Has Gon Ea been using you to experiment with his herbal concoctions again?"

Gon Ea smote the ground with his staff. "I have not. No more of this nonsense – let's go."

Nick watched the tattoos stretch across his hands as he clenched them, then straightened his spine. He was Tok Ma; he belonged here. He knew this woman, who obviously loved him as he did her, yet somehow, he could not remember her name in this other life he now inhabited.

They walked through the streets side by side, Tok Ma trying his best to sense which way she would turn at the crossroads they came upon, for he had no idea where they lived. As he agonized and racked his brains to pull her name from the recesses of his mind, Gon Ea shuffled from behind, coming to his rescue.

"Lu An, you walk too fast for an old man to keep up. I want to thank you. The people respect you and listened."

"That man was a rabble rouser," she replied.

"No match for you. At least we have three days. That's better than charging an army of trained killers and ending up with our heads on pikes."

"Where is the simurgh?" she asked.

"On the highest cliff of the Crown of Heaven." Gon Ea pointed to the Kunlun in the distance with his staff. "At the top grows the tree called Turu. It is as old as the world. The miraculous bird lives in a nest in the highest boughs. It is the spawn of Saeta, the dreamer of worlds. Its name is Fenghuang, and it is thousands of years old and can foretell the future. It is the friend of those who walk in the light, and the enemy of those who do not. Do not fear it, Tok Ma."

Lu An turned into a narrow alleyway. Gon Ea remained in the road.

"Won't you have supper with us?" she asked.

"Thanks, but no. I must be on my way. Be safe my friend."

"I'll be careful," said Tok Ma.

Lu An led the way down a row of dwellings, all nearly indistinguishable from one another, having been dug from the top down of the same hard brown earth. They walked for a while beneath the logs of overhanging thatched roofs and came to a doorway with a pattern of interlocking squares and circles carved above the wooden lintel, designating this to be the house of Ma. She swung open the door.

"How is Set?" Lu An asked their daughter, Tia, who was scooping out melons and cleaning the seeds on the table.

Tia looked up from her chore. "He has been crying. I don't know if he misses you, or is just hungry."

"He is past his feeding time. Build up the fire, Tia. I'll make us all something to eat."

Lu An picked up her son, waddled in a reed cradle, and suckled him. Tok Ma ruthlessly pulled things from baskets that he would need for his journey the next day. He brought an earthen vase to the table and spilled out a handful of blue stones, then put them in his pouch with the bone. As he worked, Tia watched him pack. "Where are you going, Father?"

"The mountains, for a few days. You help your mother while I'm gone."

"But what are the stones for?"

"I'm not sure," her father replied, rubbing his chin. "I'm told Fenghuang is fond of them – perhaps they will aid his digestion."

"Who is Fenghuang?"

Tok Ma smiled patiently. "*What is Fenghuang* is a better question. Fenghuang is a giant bird as old as the mountains that knows everything. I'm going to ask it some questions."

He gave her a hug, the familial bonds of his past life finally returning in a surge of emotions that overwhelmed him.

"Why are you crying, Father?"

"Because I love you so much."

"Love makes us stronger, Husband," said Lu An, gently rocking their son.

"It is the greatest strength," he replied.

❧

He rose before dawn the next morning, kissing them each before leaving. He had to pass below Lord Xie Pu's palace on his way to the mountains and decided to go on foot instead of horseback to avoid detection. He made his way through the tall grass a few hundred yards below the gardens in the darkness. Sentry towers were placed along the walls of the palace and on the perimeters of the gardens. Several wagons carrying cages filled with peasants passed through a gate in the wall. A regular, low pitched pounding and breathing sound came from inside, and he dreaded to think what its source may be. Tok Ma got on his belly and snaked himself along.

When he reached the plain, the sun began to rise. He pulled the hood of his cloak over his head, blending in with the terrain. It was noon when he reached the base of the mountain where the river began, fed from the falling waters. As he looked about the mountainside, he noticed a crevice where he could climb obscured by the mists of the falls.

He was known for uncanny endurance and physical prowess, but at times the climb taxed the limits of his strength. Often, he had to scale granite cliffs, straining with finger and toe to hold on.

The halfway point had not been reached when night fell. There was a rustling nearby behind a boulder. When Tok Ma turned in the direction of the noise, a hopping, one-legged boy rushed out at him talking so fast and loud that he could not understand what it was saying. It was a Shanxiao, whose naked flesh was gray and putrid, shouting curses. Tok Ma put out his palm and yelled "Ch'i." The mountain spirit hopped backward on its one leg, disappearing into the darkness.

Tok Ma tied himself to a tree growing out from the barren rocks of a crevice to keep from falling down the mountainside in his sleep. The mountains helped him remember who he was. It was coming back to him in pieces, like the attack from the Shanxiao; he remembered, without thinking, how to send it away.

He opened his pouch and pulled out the rib bone, turning it over in his hand. How many times had he walked the earth before? What was the extent of its power? How many worlds were there yet to be explored? Being Tok Ma, he realized, was the key to understanding; thoughts just get in the way.

He closed his eyes and dreamed he became an eagle, riding updrafts of warm air, gliding with ease to the top of Turu and setting down in a nest of branches and saplings.

At dawn he awoke sore and hungry and untied himself. Looking down at the river basin, Xie Pu's palace was a tiny speck. Gon Ea had said he would teach him how to change into any animal he chose, but every time he asked to be shown, the old sorcerer told him 'not now.' He wished he could turn into an eagle as he began climbing once more. At least he didn't have to worry about being seen, he was too far up, and could take an easier route.

Finally he neared the summit, an overhang of solid granite. Tok Ma wedged his feet into small outcroppings, pushing himself upward, then pulling with his hands and sliding inches at a time. The wind was fierce as it swept up the face of the mountain. Humbled by its vastness, he held on tighter, knowing it didn't care if he made it or not and ended up as a pile of bones at the bottom.

As he pulled himself over the precipice he looked about upon the enchanted paradise of Xuanpu, inhabited by spirits and Queen Mother of the West, Xiwangmu. Crawling to safety, he cast his bundle to the side and lay on his back. Turu, the sacred tree of the world, loomed above him. The wind became gentle, filled with the scent of odiferous flowers growing everywhere. When his strength returned, he sat up cross-legged and spilled the blue stones on the ground. Tok Ma began to rock back and forth.

"Fenghuang, are you there? Fenghuang, come to me," he chanted.

His hunger and exhaustion made him lightheaded and he returned to his dream, becoming an eagle, soaring atop Turu, settling on a giant nest in its lofty boughs.

His hair began streaming, blown by a sudden gust of wind.

"Nicholas," said a voice like the one in the desert storm.

He lifted his arm to protect himself from what he perceived to be a monstrous apparition. The giant bird towered above him. Its feet were golden, as was its beak, which was long enough to swallow a man in one gulp. The feathers were purplish and iridescent with flames running through them. As the simurgh turned to face him, hot licks of colored flame poured from its back; holy yellows, joyous shades of orange, energy reds.

"Are you Fenghuang?" Nick asked.

"You and I go back a long way; don't you remember me, Tok Ma?"

"After I passed through the hole in the bone I'm not sure who I am. I remember only pieces."

"Some memories are better left forgotten."

"You know I'm Nick Taylor in another life?"

"Yes. That is why I brought you here and know why you seek me out in this one. Tok Ma and Nicholas are the same soul, just in two different bodies at different times. You possess the extra rib, the mark of a shaman. You will have many different lives, changing your sheath when you find the courage. There are great powers inside you, and I will awaken them. You think you are seeking my help, but it is I who needs yours. For you to understand, I must help you remember. Do you want to know?"

"Help me understand."

The blue stones caught Fenghuang's eye. The bird cooed with appreciation and swallowed them down. The flames and colors of its plumage intensified. "Understanding is not simple. Destruction and creation are necessary to one another. The energy of the universe seeks to find balance and changes form to maintain harmony. Xie Pu threatens that harmony by serving the dark forces. He has built a palace of the afterlife in the caverns below us by enslaving the flesh of earthly life, but he will enslave the spirits of his subjects for the afterlife as well. He is preparing, even now, to steal the souls of all Shamadù and make them serve him in the hallows of the Kunlun for eternity. We must fight together to undo the wrong and restore harmony. Climb on my back."

Tok Ma mounted Fenghuang. With a few beats of its wings they climbed into the air and flew from the cliff. The vastness of creation spoke through his senses. He was amazed at the clarity and range of his vision, as though he had the eyes of an eagle. Colors took on a great deepness of hue and objects were observed in a fineness of detail at distances that were not possible for a man. The wind was alive with sounds and voices that carried a thousand stories to his ears. He began to remember his past lives, descending from the nest in Turu back to earth as a human more than once.

"I gave you the power of insight," said Fenghuang. "All your senses are amplified. Feel the earth turn, listen to the voice of knowledge in the wind."

Tok Ma's hair and clothes streamed with the long tongues of flames which blazed from the bird's wings and tail, yet he was not consumed.

"Look into the desert beneath us; the footprints of time are below its surface; sagas of love sought, battles fought. There is joy and sorrow there. Below is The Lost City of Shamadù, the one the archaeologists and scientists cannot find. Shamadù was an unknown village in the desert before the Tokloks arrived," the bird recounted.

"Beyond the Kunlun lay the kingdom of Taxila. The king of Taxila sent his soldiers over the mountains to invade Xinjiang, attacking towns along the Silk Road. When emperor Xia Yu Di in the East could endure the threat no longer, he dispatched an army of foot soldiers to drive them out of Shamadù.

"The Taxilans sent out a band of soldiers on foot to bait Yu Di's army in the desert. They let the Xia pass through their lines, feigning defeat. The Xia thought they had won a victory, but the Taxilans regrouped in the desert behind them. Taxilan horse soldiers rode out through the gates of the city of Shamadù to meet the enemy, trapping the Xia army between their two lines. Emperor Yu Di's army was slaughtered. The heads of the leaders, including Yu Di's general, were placed on pikes along the road as a warning against future attack.

"When Emperor Yu Di learned of this, he became enraged and obsessed with retaking Shamadù. He had heard rumors of celestial horses in the West that were faster and stronger than any other on earth; Toklok horses. Yu Di decided to build a cavalry, so he sent emissaries to find your people.

"They offered great riches to raise the horses for the emperor. Emperor Yu Di promised those Tokloks who came to Shamadù they would always be generously rewarded as long as they were loyal to his family. Having struck the bargain, your ancestors raised thousands of horses for Yu Di's cavalry. Yu Di used his mounted army to destroy the Taxilans.

"After his great victory, the emperor sent engineers to irrigate the land with the river and built the palace for his brother, Xie Pu's great grandfather. Shamadù became fertile and prosperous. The Tokloks raised horses for the emperors ever since."

Tok Ma put his lips to Fenghuang's ear, hidden beneath the feathers. "But what of Xie Pu? He has made us slaves; steals our daughters. We are poor now that he takes the fruits of our labors."

"A bad time is coming for Shamadù. Unless he is stopped, he will reign over the dead in the afterlife, feeding on their souls to sustain him. It will be up to you to stop him."

Chapter Six:

Lord Xie Pu

Tok Ma was puzzled. "What is it you need of me?"

"I shall explain," said Fenghuang, flying low over the palace. "Xie Pu is a dark spirit. He snatched the scepter from his father's hand as the old king's eyes were closing in death, dishonoring him, so great was his impatience to be ruler. Before the gates of the tomb of his father were shut and sealed, he stole the treasures for his father's afterlife and hid them in the mountain. Everyone used to transport the treasure was killed to prevent the secret from being told."

"What good is it if not used to good purpose?" asked Tok Ma.

The bird ruffled his neck feathers in indignation. "It sits useless, a monument to his greed. He hordes it for the glory of his own afterlife. He has been building his palace of the world-beyond for years in the caverns of the Kunlun, below the roots of the tree Turu.

"Knowing the way of tomb robbers, he had his engineers devise an underground passageway from his palace to the mountains so that no one can find it. It is an underground highway of dragon red marble decorated with the spoils and wealth of Xinjiang. At the end of this marble road lies his burial chamber, a fantastic cathedral beyond contemplation. Lord Xie Pu's sepulcher is there, encrusted with precious jewels, bathing in the light of a thousand crystals. When the old necromancer departs this life, he will be placed in the sepulcher, and his priests and the souls of his slaves sealed in his tomb to serve and feed him."

Tok Ma shook his head in bewilderment. "But why have you brought me here from a future life? Does this mean he will be victorious? Is it inescapable and nothing can change what will be?"

"You are fortunate that you are not able to remember completely. It is really a kindness. In the chaos of creation there are opposing forces playing against one another until balance is attained, and it may take more than one lifetime to understand and bring them into harmonious alignment."

Fenghuang landed by the lake where Tok Ma had been walking with Gon Ea. "I am more lost than before. Will I be victorious or not?" asked the wizard, sliding from its back.

"You have asked, so I must tell. All will seem lost, but the future holds the key. The day will come when the wrong shall be set right." The bird cocked its head to one side and regarded

Tok Ma impassively. "If we get outside of our little worlds and observe what is really happening around us, and also within us, if we really look, we shall see that it is selfishness that causes all the harm and pain in the world. (Credit to Buddhadasa Bhik-khu; *The Burden of Selfishness*.) Selfishness is a great burden, and you must let it go. In your first life, here in Shamadù, you chose your own life above that of others, and failed. In your life as Nick, you are on the same path. To save Shamadù, you must let go of self-interest completely. You have been given a second chance."

Tok Ma huffed indignantly. "Is that why I am here – for a second chance? Do you know what you ask?" Fenghuang rose into the air. "Wait, I have more questions." Tok Ma watched the bird recede in the distance. He walked back to Shamadù as night fell, arriving home in the dark.

Lu An lit a lamp and was dismayed by what she saw in his face. "Why so glum?"

He smiled back sadly. "Fenghuang brought bad tidings. Lord Xie Pu has been taking the innocent under false promises of reward. We must expose him to the people and warn them; tell them to flee. We fear Xie Pu in life, but in death he is worse. It seems he thinks he can take his wealth and glory with him to the afterlife - and our souls, too." Tok Ma shook his head. "Tokloks do not need servants and trinkets in the next life. There is no need for sacrifice."

"Sacrifice – of us? Is that why your thoughts are so grim?"

The tattoos moved about Tok Ma's face as it settled into a scowl. "Lord Xie Pu will take as many as he can to serve him after death. Fenghuang says he will die soon and the only way to escape his plan is to leave Shamadù. Time is short and we must prepare to save as many as we can."

"Can it really be so bad? Tell me everything from the beginning."

Tok Ma recounted the events of his journey and all that Fenghuang had revealed to him, leaving out the part about his second chance.

Lu An looked at their children sleeping near the fire. "What are we to do?"

"Return to our homeland. Those who return will live. Those who don't will be his slaves in the underworld."

"Never. This is our home."

He took her by the shoulders, looking into her eyes. "Yes. We must leave Shamadù forever."

"I would sooner fight to the death." She turned her back on him and sat by her son's cradle.

❧

In the early morning, the people gathered together in the square. Lu An, Gon Ea, the elders, and Tok Ma, faced them from beneath the awning. Gon Ea held up his staff to quiet the crowd.

"People of Shamadù, Tok Ma has returned from the Crown of Heaven and spoken with Fenghuang."

Tok Ma stepped forward, pointing over the rooftops to the palace. "Shamadù has been our home for many generations, but we cannot be loyal any longer to Lord Xie Pu: the trust is broken. Fenghuang has foretold the earthly reign of Lord Xie Pu is coming to an end." The wizard explained what was told him to the crowd.

"You see, I said so," said the merchant. "We must sharpen our swords and put them to the blade first!"

The crowd began chanting "death to the Xia."

"No, no," shouted Tok Ma, raising his arms. "I know how in your hearts you want to defend your homes and families, that is only natural, but you don't understand. There is no way to prevail against a well-trained army. Gather your loved ones and belongings - prepare to depart at once, there is no time to waste."

Lu An turned from the crowd to face her husband. "Tok Ma, I have always stood by your side, but I must ask, if there is so little time, then surely, mustn't we take up the sword now?"

Tok Ma spoke loudly so all would hear. "If we do, the Emperor of Xia -and his generals will come to the aid of his cousin, Lord Xie Pu. In effect, it would do Xie Pu's work for him."

An elder pulled Tok Ma aside. "How much time do we have?" he asked. "To a creature as old as Fenghuang, a day is like a thousand years."

"Fenghuang said it will start when Lord Xie Pu crosses over.' How and exactly when he will die, I do not know."

The elder conferred with the council members and a heated debate ensued. Finally, he turned to the crowd: "The council has decided. Children and women and those who cannot fight; collect all the food and water you can carry and be ready to leave in five days. All those who are strong enough to fight; sharpen your swords, gather your horses, and stand ready to defend them." He motioned Tok Ma aside. "Tok Ma...."

Tok Ma turned to face him.

"You are to seek audience with Lord Xie Pu at once. See how much longer the necromancer might last. Most importantly, learn exactly how he will carry out his intentions and when he shall begin this evil perfidy."

Tok Ma bowed in affirmation.

As he and Lu An walked home, Gon Ea accompanied them. "What did the elder want to know?" he asked.

Tok Ma frowned. "He wants me to meet Xie Pu to learn how and when this will happen."

"He could die any day now. When is the last time anyone has seen him in public?" said Lu An.

"She has a point," said Gon Ea. "It's been over a year."

"The elders are right. I must see him for myself. Perhaps he'll die in a fortnight or perhaps it may be years. But to know his plans and how he will accomplish them; that is no easy task. To gain his ear is even harder."

Lu An pulled Tok Ma's sleeve and they all stopped together in the alley. "Forgive me for speaking against you. It's just that it is so hard to accept what we must do. But I love you and will always be at your side."

Tok Ma took her in his arms and kissed her. "I will love you until the end of time."

"That long? Are you sure?"

Gon Ea waited patiently, then spoke. "I know how to get an audience with him. Bring him a gift he can't refuse; ox bones. Lord Xie Pu is a prognosticator. He is obsessed with reading the oracle bones. Ox shoulder blades are best."

Tok Ma beamed. "You are right."

"Gon Ea, you are a genius," said Lu An. "There is a pit of ox carcasses by the burial mound. We will gather up as many shoulder bones as we can carry as an offering of devotion to him and ask for a divination."

"Then it is decided," said Gon Ea. "Tok Ma and I shall go tomorrow."

"It is not decided," said Lu An. "I'm going, too."

Tok Ma regarded her sternly. "Lu An, you will stay. It's very dangerous. There is no telling what he will do."

"I will decide for myself, and I am going."

"We need her," said Gon Ea. "It will seem less suspicious if she comes."

"All right," Tok Ma conceded. "This is not the time to argue."

They returned to the house and prepared for their visit to

the palace. Lu An emptied several baskets onto the table and stacked them on the floor by the front door. "Two baskets of shoulder bones should make him happy," said Gon Ea. After dinner, he took his leave, agreeing to meet at the burial mound in the morning.

"Where is our homeland?" asked Lu An. "I thought it was here."

Tok Ma sighed. "It has been so long. In the plains past Samarkland."

"What is happening, Father?" asked Tia. "Where are we going?"

"We're going to find a new home with a better life. You may make some new friends."

"Just us? Where?"

Tok Ma pulled a stool up beside her at the table. "All the Tokloks in Shamadù. To our ancestors in the west, if they will take us back. Maybe you'll find a boyfriend there. Do you know the story of the fish and the bird? An old fisherman told it to me."

She wrinkled her nose and shook her head. "It's not about boyfriends, is it?"

He nodded his head solemnly. "One day a bird flew over the lake, hoping to find a tasty meal. She was flying low, when suddenly a handsome fish with shining scales jumped high and cried, "marry me.""

Tia laughed. "She can't live in the water."

Her father continued with a smile. "As she flew away, no one else came to mind, but the handsome fish and the words of love she was leaving behind. Suddenly she turned. 'We can never marry,' she said, 'our worlds are far apart, but why cruel fish, have you stolen my heart?' Then he leapt in the air, and spoke these words that are true:

> *'At night when the lake is still*
> *And the moon shines over the hill,*
> *The water becomes a mirror;*
> *In its reflection, our worlds draw near*
> *Promise that you'll meet me there,*
> *Promise you'll not forget*
> *If your love is as true as mine*
> *Nothing will keep us apart;*
> *We can live in both worlds with only one heart'"*

The next morning they had to look their best to go to the palace. Lu An wore her finest hat with colored feathers and a fur coat. Tok Ma wore a finely woven coat with tight stitching around the collars and a brightly colored belt of spun wool. They saddled their horses and rode to the outskirts of Shamadù to a burial mound from which sprouted tall posts hewn from trees. Sitting on top each post was an ox skull and below that flew colorful cloth flags. The hides of the oxen were used to wrap the coffins for protection before burial in the mound. The left-over oxen remains, along with the bones, were buried in a pit nearby. They skirted the cemetery respectfully and rode to a depression in the ground.

Lu An and Tok Ma dismounted by the pit where Gon Ea was waiting for them. Lu An removed a shovel from her horse and dug in the loose soil. The men began digging with their hands until the jumbled bones of the beasts were exposed. She pointed to a large white shoulder bone. "Like this one. Only the white ones." Soon their baskets were full.

They made a handsome threesome as they rode to the king's palace. The palace walls appeared small at first in the distance, then slowly grew as they approached, stretching for half a mile in each direction.

"There is an entrance on the other side where I saw them take in a cart load of people. Something unrighteous is going on in there," said Tok Ma. "I heard strange pounding and breathing sounds from inside."

The gates were made of intricately decorated brass plates. Soldiers were posted along the top of the walls, which were made of hewn trees. A sentry stepped out from behind a hidden door in the wall and greeted them.

"State your business," he ordered.

"We are Toklok elders with a gift for Lord Xie Pu," said Tok Ma.

The sentry rummaged through the baskets. "Bones?" he asked.

"Ox bones. We are told he is fond of them," said Lu An.

He disappeared through the wall for several minutes, then opened the gate. "Enter. The secretary will see you."

"Please tell him we are here to see Lord Xie Pu," said Lu An.

"The Grand Secretary is a she. You must say Madam Secretary in her presence."

As the gate shut behind them, they were told to dismount, and a soldier took the horses' reins. He led them along the main path as the eyes of the soldiers on the walls followed them suspiciously. Ahead of them lay the great palace; five stories of intricately carved teak, brought from the distant forests of Xia. The roof was covered in fine colored tiles of red, green, and blue, and the beams protruding from the roof hips were carved into dragons. Gardens tended by slaves surrounded the palace. Paths wound their way through trees, ponds, and exotic flowers up to the palace entrance where several soldiers stood guard.

Wu Shi Zan'er, secretary and concubine to Lord Xie Pu, greeted them at the entrance doorway. They were led to a waiting room and seated. "Lord Xie Pu is pleased and thanks you for your thoughtful gift."

"We are honored, Madam Secretary," said Tok Ma.

The secretary smiled and poured each a cup of tea. "Tell me your names and what it is you wish to discuss, so I may be of assistance."

Tok Ma introduced his companions and himself. "We wish to know what the coming season will bring and if there will be enough rain to grow the crops. We wish to inquire about the horses and if there will be enough to feed them this year. Perhaps Lord Xie Pu will be gracious enough to bestow his blessings on us."

Wu Shi bowed politely. "He is with his generals now and may take some time. I am sorry, you must be patient, but I will call you when he can speak with you. Please wait here."

"Do not drink the tea," said Gon Ea, wrinkling his nose when she had left.

"They will be offended if we don't," said Lu An. She raised her cup to her lips.

He pointed to the corner. "Poison. Pour it out over there."

"Do you hear that noise?" asked Tok Ma.

Lu An returned to the table and set her empty cup down. "What is it?"

"It comes from the building behind the garden, near where the carts go in. I'm going to take a look."

"I'll go with you," said Gon Ea.

"No, I must go alone. Make up some excuse if Wu Shi comes."

Lu An held him tightly for a moment, then he disappeared quietly through the door.

He heard the voices of the king and his generals in the throne room and quickly made his way to the end of the hall where he found the servants' passage and entered. He came upon an exit and stepped outside into the gardens. Guards were posted along the outer walls of the courtyard, but they faced outward, staring over the fields like automatons. A loud pounding sound followed by a noise like an exhalation from a giant lung came from the building at the far end of the gardens. Strolling brazenly, as though he had every right in the world to be there, he approached the mysterious structure and entered the open gate.

The interior was dim and lit by torchlight. At the far end was the opening to a shaft descending obliquely into the earth. Beside the entrance was a great bellows operated by six men pulling in unison on a handle to the beat of a taigu drum. Slaves carrying baskets of rocks strapped to their backs emerged from the tunnel. To evade detection, Tok Ma turned sideways and slid along the walls to a chamber. He peered inside and ducked in the doorway. The enormous room was filled with jade congs: hexagonal columns about three and a half feet high and decorated with monster eyes and mouths, crowned with libation bowls. At the far end of the room two priests stood by the corpse of a young girl on a concave marble altar, draining her blood into the top of one of the congs.

The air was thick with the smell of death and the mouse nest reek of mushquat root used to induce a dream-like stupor until the heart stopped beating. He could not fight the choking feeling. He gagged, not from the stench in his nostrils, but from the abomination he was witnessing. Looking over a cong, he realized the priests had seen him and were nodding to someone. A hand from behind clamped a wadded cloth over his mouth and nose and he fought to hold his breath, but could not. The pounding of the taigu receded. A thick fog floated over his consciousness, covering him in a blanket of silence.

ↄ

He felt a kick in his ribs and rolled over painfully on the floor, looking up at the time worn face of Lord Xie Pu. He struggled to rise and shake the fog from his mind. Xie Pu kicked him down again. Tok Ma twisted his head and saw Lu An and Gon Ea held at sword point by two guards.

"I'm sorry to keep you waiting so long, Tok Ma, especially after receiving your kind gift. Wu Shi tells me you are asking for my blessing. I am always flattered to be asked, but that is not what I have in mind for you and your companions." Xie Pu nodded to a guard who pulled the sorcerer to his feet. Wu Shi stepped behind Lu An to take the guard's place and pressed a dagger into her neck.

"Lord Xie Pu, we came to show our good will. I took a walk in the garden and heard the noise."

Xie Pu ran his finger down his nose. "Do not incur my wrath, liar. You did more than just take a walk. You are here spying, not on an act of good will. Who sent you?"

A thin ribbon of red flowed down Lu An's neck as Wu Shi pressed in her dagger more deeply. "Let them go and I will tell you," he said.

"You are not in a position to bargain." Xie Pu nodded to Wu Shi, and the ribbon widened. Lu An gasped. "It would be a shame to kill her," said Wu Shi.

Tok Ma folded his arms and bowed his head low in submission. "Lord, I will tell you." Wu Shi released the dagger from Lu An's neck.

"I'm waiting," said Xie Pu.

Tok Ma raised his head and blew a handful of red powder into the air, which exploded in a cloud of light. He pushed Lu An and Gon Ea into the cloud, leaving Wu Shi and the others blinded and empty handed.

"Guards!" shouted Xie Pu.

Tok Ma pulled the sword from the nearest guard's hand, then ran them both through. He advanced on Xie Pu, swinging the sword at his neck, but the blade only sliced the air. Tok Ma looked about wildly for the king, then felt Wu Shi's dagger in his back. As she pushed it into his heart, he fell to his knees, swaying.

Lord Xie Pu reappeared before him, sneering. "A sorcerer? I don't think so, at least not a very good one."

Wu Shi shouted through the court doorway, "Don't let them escape!"

A moment later Lu An and Gon Ea were dragged back in with their hands tied behind their backs.

"Take them to the priests," ordered Xie Pu. "As for you, Tok Ma, I will drain your carcass myself."

"Murderer!" cried Lu An.

Tok Ma mustered one last grain of strength and pulled the bone from his pouch. "Es tālum wasāleem tú bashar nékè," he sputtered, and found his way through the hole.

Chapter Seven:

Hot and Sour Soup

NICK OPENED HIS EYES and felt his side where it had been torn by the fall into the tomb. Bandages covered hardened scabs and stitching. He lifted his hands to his face, and the tattoos were gone.

"Mr. Taylor, how are you feeling?" said the doctor, writing on a clipboard at the foot of the bed.

Nick tried to speak, but nothing came out. The nurse stopped adjusting the intravenous tubes and brought him a glass of ice water, which he gulped greedily. "My tongue is sticking to the roof of my mouth, my head is splitting, and everything is hazy."

The doctor pulled up Nick's lids and examined his eyes, which were bloodshot and swollen. "Your eyes should clear up in a day or so. I have some drops that will help, otherwise it looks like you are improving nicely."

"When can I get out of here?"

"In a few days. You need rest while we run a few more tests. You had hypothermia from being in that tomb and were beginning to freeze dry," he said with a wry smile. "This is going to be a shock, but you were on life support until this morning. You've been in a coma for five days."

"Five days? I was in Shamadù."

"Yes, that is where they found you."

"The Lost City of ancient Shamadù."

The doctor smiled. "Get some rest."

"Doctor, will you please contact Michael Chou at the Xinjiang Regional Museum and let him know I'm alright?"

"He's been here several times and called every day. We'll let him know. Xiuxi – rest. And one more thing, Mr. Taylor."

"What's that?"

"Stay out of the desert for a while."

Nick crossed his fingers beneath the sheet and nodded. "Xing bu xing."

At the end of the week, the doctor checked him over and okayed the discharge. Michael and Ann Lee picked him up in the morning from the hospital lobby. Ann Lee gave Nick a hug. "Troublemaker," she teased.

"I'm sorry for the mess I dragged you into. Michael, I can't thank you enough for rescuing me. Are you going to fire me?"

Michael laughed. "I have to tell you, Nick, I didn't think

we would find anything for months, but you found the tomb in three days. How did you do it, some sort of gut feeling?"

"No, not a gut feeling – more like something I felt in my bones." As he smiled, a new crack opened on his lip.

"Let's get you in the car. You will stay with us until you get back on your feet."

"I'm okay. If you take me to my apartment, that will be fine."

"That is ridiculous. This is not a matter for you to decide," said Ann Lee. "You will stay with us until you are on your feet again."

They drove toward an area of the city called Shayibak. Michael noticed Ann Lee frowning in the rear-view mirror. "I have to put up with her every day," he said. "She's right, though."

"What happened to my suitcase? Most of my clothes were in it," said Nick.

"Xue brought it back in your Land Rover. It's at our house," said Ann Lee.

Nick let out a sigh of relief. "That's a load off. I had put some maps and the phone number of a fellow named Jih-Wen Chang in it. He may be able to get us some laborers for excavations."

"Good thinking. I'm not sure how many people we can get from the university and we can only spare a few from the museum," said Michael.

"Nick," said Ann Lee, "do you remember anything from the coma? Is it all a blank?"

Nick shut his eyes, grimacing. "I can remember most of it. There were some good things and some bad things. Some of it would be better forgotten." His shoulders bunched and he leaned over. Ann Lee reached over the seat and patted his back. "It's okay, Nick. I shouldn't have asked, I'm sorry."

"No, I'm the one who needs to apologize. But it was so real - like the most vivid dream I ever had, like another life in a different world. You'll never believe me if I tried to tell you. And Tia, and Lu An, they're still back there. I must go back."

Ann Lee and Michael exchanged glances in the mirror. "It's okay, Nick. You are back. Take it easy, everything's fine."

Nick folded himself into a ball and rocked back and forth in his seat. They arrived at the underground garage at the condominium. Michael parked and held the car door open for several minutes until Nick uncurled and got out.

As Ann Lee set out dinner on the table, Michael shoved a bowl in front of Nick. "Try this smoked duck."

Nick began shoveling it down and everything else in sight. "God, I'm starving. This is really delicious."

Ann Lee looked at Michael. "How come you don't appreciate my cooking like that?"

"I love your cooking. It's just that I haven't gone five days without eating."

"Seriously, you are very lucky, Michael," said Nick, smiling at Ann Lee. "I'm ready for a workout. What's in the hot and sour soup?"

Ann Lee filled Nick's cup with tea. "Wood ear. It's a fungus that improves circulation. It's an ancient health cure."

"It's better than penicillin." Nick sipped from his cup while peering at Michael inquisitively. "Now that we have the tomb and the mummies, did you get some backers for the project?"

"No money yet, but I got the ear of *National Geographic* and *Discovery Channel*. When they heard of your accident and what you found, they agreed to do a story on the tomb. I'm meeting with CCTV and the BBC tomorrow to see if they want to get in on it, too. Best of all, John Mohr has agreed to lend us Gail Norton. I'm glad you suggested her. She will be arriving next week to coordinate the satellite imaging."

"Agh", said Nick, cracking his lip again. "That is very good news." He dabbed it with his napkin."

"Your accident was a stroke of luck."

"How did you find me, Michael?"

Michael poured more tea. "It wasn't me. Xue called the police, who could do nothing until the storm ended three days later. They went to see a local named Ehmet who insisted that his son lead the search. His son found your hat half buried in the sand. Two days later he found the tip of a beam from the burial chamber exposed from the storm. They said the mummies looked better than you did when they found you."

"Ehmet must be the old man I met at the café. I wouldn't be here if it wasn't for him and his son. So, how did I get to Urumqi?"

"The police flew you here by helicopter to Friendship Hospital. When I checked in on you, they weren't sure you were going to make it. The hypothermia slowed down your heart, not to mention the dehydration. You know the rest."

"I think it must have been horrible for you being down there for so long," said Ann Lee. "You had no light or water. Just mummies. The mind can play tricks on you."

Nick exhaled slowly. "Yes, it can play tricks on you. I had the most amazing dream about living in The Lost City." He glanced from Ann Lee to Michael with a bewildered look. "The scientist in me says it was a hallucination, but some other part says it's true. I don't believe it is something that can be explained with cause and effect."

"I think it seems real to you," said Michael. "Do you mind talking about it?"

He swirled the tea in his cup, collecting his thoughts, then looked up at Michael. "It didn't really start with finding the tomb. It started after you called me back in the States."

Nick began with his dream about the shaman the night after the Blue Baby arrived. Michael and Ann Lee listened quietly until he finished his story by ending with Xie Pu and the hole in the bone and waking up in the hospital.

"That really blows my mind," Michael said. "I'm amazed at some of the details you have given. Interestingly enough, they seem scientifically plausible at times, but most of it is just the stuff dreams are made of."

Ann Lee frowned impatiently. "Wait a minute, Michael. You can't discredit everything just like that. We dream in metaphors. Just because something is a metaphor doesn't mean it's not true."

"Thank you, Ann Lee. The artists run ahead of the pack. I'm glad you believe me," said Nick. "I have a proposition to make that could help us find The Lost City and the tomb of Xie Pu."

"Him again - Xie who?" asked Michael. "We can't start digging without scientific justification. This all costs money. We need proof."

"You remind me of someone – I won't say who. I know you don't believe any of it, but just hear me out."

"I'm still listening," said Michael.

"We don't need coordinates for the tomb now that we know where it is. That will save expense. We can give Gail the coordinates for an area just to the east of the dried lakebed of Shamadù and ask her to have her NASA buddies run a scan of that area at maximum depth. When she runs the analysis on the data from the scan, there will be an indication that something is under there, and we will have enough reason to start excavating."

"There is more science to that and there will be proof. I like it," said Michael. "As long as it doesn't cost him anything, Mohr will probably agree to it. You and Xue go back to the tomb in Shamadù. Set up a camp and walk the land for the coordinates to give to Gail. I will find students from the university to assist you with that. But we do two scans, one around the tomb, and one near the dry lakebed where you say The Lost City lies."

Nick smiled triumphantly. "I promise you it's under there."

ᦿ

When Nick and the team pulled into Shamadù three days later, they parked in front of the café where he and Xue had stopped before. The bleary-eyed waiter ran over to Nick, saying something in Uyghur.

Xue translated. "He says, 'I didn't think you would be back, good to see you.'"

"Ask him if Mr. Ehmet is here, will you?" said Nick.

"He says he hasn't seen him for a few days," said Xue. "He asks, 'what do you want to eat?'"

After dinner Nick drove them to the guesthouse. He pulled out the map of the desert of Shamadù from his travel bag, unrolled it on one of the beds, and pointed to a spot near the location of the Charbashi ruins. "We'll start here tomorrow. The tomb is about 400 meters from the ruins. We'll erect a yurt over the tomb and another to shelter visitors and the media. The camp should be set up by the end of the day. Then we walk the land."

"What about thieves?" asked Ma Cheng, one of the two students Michael had picked for the team.

"The County of Qiemo has provided a guard for the tomb until the site has been established," said Xue.

Drawing a box around an area just outside the dried up lakebed of Shamadù, Nick explained to Ma Cheng and Hu Song, also from the university, that they all would walk an area of about one hundred square kilometers between the four of them over the course of two weeks, noting the latitude and longitude of mounds or depressions, and any ruins. When they were sure of the area for exploration, the coordinates would be sent to Michael Chou for satellite imaging. Michael would then get permission from the central government and relay them to Gail Norton in Philadelphia to pass on to her friends at NASA Worldview-2.

"We better check in with Michael," said Xue. He handed his phone to Nick.

Back in Urumqi, Michael picked up as he sat down to diner. "How are you making out?"

"We just went over the plans for tomorrow. The weather is fine this time; we'll start setting up camp tomorrow."

"That is great. Yesterday I released pictures of the tomb and the story about the discovery to the BBC, CCTV, and CNBC. John Mohr saw it online and called me. We are good on the satellite imaging and he said Gail can stay as long as we need her. He was for it all the time, of course."

"Maybe he's not the worst person in the world, after all."

"Nick," said Michael, pausing. "He said he wants to bury the hatchet. He respects you on a professional level, but he had to do what he had to do, not because he wanted to."

"I'm glad you told me that."

"Hey, it's in a good cause. By the way, there will be a press conference that will include *National Geographic* and *Discover Magazine.* Gail will be giving a presentation on radar imaging at the conference."

"You are a genius," said Nick.

"I want you to talk about how you found the tomb. Just the facts and the science."

"I get it."

❧

The following morning the yurts were pitched. The camp was complete with a communications center and mess hall. The burial chamber was covered by a tall yurt large enough so the roof of the tomb could be partially removed, allowing onlookers to peer down inside. Nick and Xue placed the log beams of the roof beside the entrance to the chamber, then looked down on the coffin of the tall man.

"I wonder who he was," said Xue. "The way he is dressed, he must have been someone special."

Nick smiled strangely at Xue. "He is Tok Ma, an elder of Shamadù."

Xue nodded. "That sounds like a good name for him. Maybe Tocharian."

"That is his name. And he is Tocharian."

They photographed and cataloged the tomb in detail. The clothing found in the tomb was a source of excitement. The sophistication of the weave used in the cloth was beyond that which would be expected from an ancient people. The dyes used as coloring had not faded in thousands of years.

Xue asked Michael to bring in outside experts specializing in ancient weaving techniques. He hoped they would be able to trace the origins of the people buried in the tomb by studying the weave of the cloth.

Cheng and Song bombarded Nick and Xue with questions about the age of the mummies and how they came to be there in Shamadù. Nick explained he thought they were Celtic Tocharians about 3,800 years old because the Blue Baby had been found near Charbashi and had been carbon dated at that age. He made no mention of his trip to the past with the shaman and what he had learned there.

On the second day, Nick led the team from the camp to the top of a wind eroded yardang. "This is our start point and end point. You each have a map and a GPS. Note your position here. We'll walk the perimeter first, then sweep the rest in quadrants, spreading apart to get it all."

Things went faster than expected, and by the evening of the tenth day, Nick was able to send the coordinates stored in the GPSs to Michael. They spent the next few days exploring some elevated areas found during their walks. Xue and the students were surprised when Nick told them one might be the walls surrounding an ancient palace.

At the end of two weeks in the desert, they made their way back to the town of Shamadù to re-provision. After returning to the guesthouse, their first priority was to shower and have a properly cooked meal. As Nick put on a clean change of clothes, Xue held out his cell phone. "For you. It's Gail Norton," he said. "She's at the museum."

Nick grabbed the phone. "Hi Gail, I miss you."

"I miss you too. It's good to hear your voice."

"I can't wait for you to get here. You're going to love this place."

Gail waited for her phone to stop crackling. "Michael said you had an accident and were hospitalized for a while. Are you okay?"

"A fortuitous accident. I'll tell you about it later. What did the scans show?"

"It's pretty exciting. I have good news for you guys," said Gail. "The Worldview-2 images weren't clear enough, so last night we used a satellite called Aster to do infrared scans. The infrared imaging analysis shows shapes that suggest walls and buildings at about two and a half meters below the surface."

"Which set of coordinates? Near the tomb, or out to the east?" asked Nick.

"The eastern set."

Nick walked to the window and looked out over the desert. "That's the palace."

"What palace?"

"The palace is higher in elevation. The old city is below it. It's a long story. I'll explain later," said Nick.

"There must be something down there, without a doubt."

"Can you bring the images along with you for the press conference?"

"You bet," she said.

"See you soon. Have a good trip."

∾

The day of the press conference arrived quickly. Michael had planned the event with much attention to detail and had driven down in a truck loaded with equipment and supplies. A temporary helicopter pad was constructed about one hundred yards from the camp for the conference attendees. Seats were set up in the yurt and a podium was placed near the tomb. The sides of the yurt were rolled up so the ruins of Charbashi could be seen in the distance for dramatic effect.

"What do you think?" Michael asked Nick when every-thing was in place.

Nick clapped. "A standing ovation. It's quite a show." He looked down into the tomb at the sleeping figures below. "My friends, I don't think you would ever have imagined all this in your wildest dreams. I am sorry."

A large helicopter appeared over the horizon. Nick knew Gail would be on it and waited on the periphery of the landing area. When the helicopter touched down, the passenger door opened. He ran through the sandy downdraft to greet her.

The first passenger off the helicopter was not Gail, but someone Nick recognized from TV: Marie Brown from the BBC. As she walked toward Nick, she pulled out a Nikon and snapped several shots in quick succession. "Hello Mr. Taylor," she said. "I can't wait to hear about your discovery. Did you know you were on the news last night?"

It took him a moment to adjust to the sudden intrusion of the world into the peaceful desert. "I'm afraid we don't get the news out here," he replied. "We tend to be more up on the past than the present."

She laughed. "That is charming."

More members of the press and representatives of archaeological institutions from China, Europe, and the United States followed behind her. Gail was the last to walk down the ramp, lugging a knapsack in one hand and a large portfolio in the other.

"Excuse me, Marie," he said abruptly. Nick pulled Gail to him and they shared a long kiss. When he opened his eyes, Marie Brown was still holding her camera and smiling. "Okay ladies, I'll show you where you can put your things."

He guided them away from the helicopter to the press yurt. "You can leave your things here," he said. Marie walked to the edge of the burial chamber and began taking pictures.

He and Gail embraced again. "How long can you stay in Xinjiang?"

She smiled and searched his face for hidden meanings. "I'm on loan as long as I'm useful. It's kind of open ended."

"We're going to need a lot of additional scans. It's going to take a long time."

She wagged a cautionary finger. "Don't forget about the trouble you got into over spending too much money."

Nick rolled his eyes upward imploringly. "I may have ulterior motives, but you're worth it." He noticed the yurt was filling up with people. "We need to find Michael. We're going to start."

Representatives from archaeological organizations, magazines, and press corps took their seats. Michael walked behind the podium and motioned to Nick and Gail to join him. He tapped the microphone and thanked everyone for making the difficult journey to their remote outpost. Beginning with a history of exploration in Xinjiang from the early 1900s, Michael told about the exploits of the Swedish geographer, Sven Heyden, and the archaeologists, Folkman Sorenson and Aural Stein, and then explained about the resulting Chinese policy to block exploitation of the region by outsiders.

"But today the doors are open again," he told them. "A new era of international cooperation is beginning. This region is a melting pot, and home to ancient treasures from many cultures. A collaboration of scientists from all over the world is needed to discover and understand them."

Michael introduced Nick. Nick gestured to the burial chamber below him, shaking his head. "There is so much we still don't know about them: where did they come from; who are they, and where did they go? How is it that these Caucasoid people settled here in Xinjiang? I believe Dr. Chou is right. This region has been a crossroads of cultures for millennia. The past holds the key to the future. It has brought us together here today: Asians, Uyghurs, Europeans, North Americans, Africans, and Mongolians. It is our hope that we can find the answers to these riddles together."

Nick described the chain of events leading to the discovery of the burial chamber from the time of Folkman Sorenson to the time he fell in by accident. There was a great deal of laughter, and he laughed, too, despite his personal feelings. When their laughter had died down, he introduced Gail. She brought out the blowups of the tiles from the satellite radar scans suggesting ancient walls and buildings under the sand. As she explained that the burial chamber could be linked to the structures below the surface, cameras clicked and hands flew up in the air.

"Dr. Norton, can you tell us about how these images were made? Is this space archaeology?" asked a journalist from National Geographic.

"I'm happy to," said Gail. "Space archaeology has come into its own recently, thanks to advances developed by Dr. Shann Parker." Gail pointed to one of the images she had pinned to an easel. "These are called *tiles,* which are infrared snapshots taken from about 380 miles up. When they were first transmitted to us, the outlines of structures below the ground were not visible. By using a kind of special graphics software developed by Dr. Parker, I was able to create contrasts between the soils and vegetation over the buried structures and the surrounding area. The contrast reveals the contours and shapes of what's buried below that are otherwise invisible to the naked eye."

After she answered more questions about satellite remote surveillance techniques, Michael pointed to Marie Brown. "Yes, Ms. Brown."

"I have a question for Mr. Taylor. Mr. Taylor, what led you to suspect The Lost City was out there in the spot where you found it?"

Nick adjusted the mic. "There have been references to its existence in scrolls found at Jioahe and in other writings. We have long suspected it to be near the present-day city, but no one could find it. If I told you it was a lucky accident, or that it was the process of elimination because we had looked everywhere else first, you probably would have no trouble accepting that. The truth is, however, I had a dream that it was there. I know that's not scientific, but we need catalysts: visions and feelings in our bones. It was an intuitive hunch."

There were more questions. When it was over, Nick leaned over to Michael. "Are you ticked off with me about being unscientific?"

Michael sighed. "No. They liked your answer."

The remainder of the day was filled with discourse, questions, and ideas between the archaeologists and journalists. Nick circulated his theories on the origins of the mummies, explaining with conviction that they were horse herders from somewhere to the west of Samarkand, in all probability, Celtic Tocharians.

"Mr. Taylor," said a professor from Xinjiang University who had been studying the tattoos on the mummies' faces, "what do think of the tattoos? People from the tombs near Loulan have facial paintings indicating they were sun worshipers."

"We need to study them more. I'm sure these are not sun worshipers, but their time period is before the Buddha and the other organized world religions. Our ancestors back then understood the world through shamanic rituals and beliefs. The symbolism is shamanic."

Later, after the visitors had boarded the helicopter to fly back to Urumqi, Michael called everyone together. "I want to thank you for the superb job you have done. Our conference has been a success." He nodded happily to each member of the team. "The winter will be upon us soon and it will be too cold to work in the desert. We'll start excavating in the spring. Because of your excellent work, we have all the backing we need."

Chapter Eight:

The Night Market

GAIL, XUE AND NICK hiked out to the yardang the next morning to examine where the excavations would take place. Nick gave Gail a GPS and brought up their location. He pointed to the southeast; the direction of ancient Shamadù. "The old city is out there, and the palace a kilometer or so to the right."

"What makes you so sure it's a palace?" asked Gail.

"Trust me on this one."

"Trust you?"

Nick shrugged. "From the scans, of course. The images look like walls surrounding a courtyard."

Gail pulled out her binoculars and searched the empty horizon. "You never would know. How could people live out there?"

"There are records of a lake," said Xue, "perhaps ten kilometers long. At one time, there was plenty of water. What we are looking at now, was once green, can you believe it?"

"It's hard to imagine." She shook her head. "It's a whole lot of digging. That's a lot of sand."

"Definitely. Way lots," Nick agreed. "We better get back. There are mummies to pack."

☙

Michael had brought along two museum display handlers who were assembling large wooden crates and lining them with archival Tyvek when they got back to camp. The mummies would be flown to Urumqi Hospital to be examined internally by MRI and X-ray, then moved to the museum to be put on display in their coffins. As the crates were assembled, Gail, Xue and Nick documented and boxed the piles of clothing that had been found in the tomb.

Gail packed away a beret made of felt, then held up a tall conical hat with a brim. "I suppose they wanted to look good in the next life. This one looks like an alchemist's hat."

Xue laughed. "That's the one Mickey Mouse wore in *The Sorcerer's Apprentice*."

"I apologize for them, Tok Ma," said Nick. "They don't mean to be disrespectful."

Xue and Gail exchanged glances. "That's what Nick named him," said Xue.

"That is his name. Be careful with those hats. They're 3,800 years old."

"They look like they were just dry cleaned," Gail teased.

Nick rolled his eyes. "They were. Didn't you know they had already invented dry cleaning back then?"

By the end of the day Michael and the crew had packed and labelled everything in the tomb with a cross-referenced code to discourage thieves and curiosity seekers. The mummies had been secured in their coffins with Ethafoam and peanut bags and sealed in the shipping crates with tamper evident tape.

They sat together in the mess yurt to eat a dinner made of rehydrated red lentils, kale and ginger. When they had finished eating, Nick poured everyone a cup of coffee.

"What is this?" cried Xue, pouring his on the ground. "Is this what they call cowboy coffee?"

"Oh, I'm sorry, I forgot my French press," said Nick.

Michael pulled a bottle of plum brandy from his coat and un-screwed the top. "We'll have to break up the camp in the morn-ing," he said, passing the bottle to Xue. "The helicopter is going to be full with the crates and equipment, Gail. You'll go back with Nick and Xue in the Land Rover. Keep the peace, okay?"

"Sure, Michael. I still need to find a place when I get back. Do you mind if I do some apartment hunting?"

"Of course. I'm going to be tied up with the mummy test-ing at the hospital for a while. Perhaps if Nick and Xue don't kill each other, they can show you around a bit."

As night fell, Nick and Gail walked back to the far side of the yardang. The sand had eroded considerably from the wind there and they could stand unnoticed from inquisitive eyes.

"It's really cold," said Gail, shivering. What do you think the temperature is?"

"I'm not sure, but well below freezing. This is nothing. Wait until early morning." He put his arms around her and held her close. "It would be warmer in my tent." He brushed her lips with his.

After a long moment she broke away, smiling. "They're awfully old fashioned around here. I think we better not."

He pulled her close again. "I understand. Let me hold you for a minute."

"Do you love me?" she asked.

He caressed her cheek and kissed her. "Very much."

"I love you, too. In case you're wondering."

Nick sighed. "You've confirmed my suspicion."

ᴄ

It was late in the morning by the time they had hiked across the desert back to Shamadù. They threw their backpacks into the back of the Land Rover. Gail wanted to take in the ruins at Niya on the way back to Urumqi, but it was starting to get dark as they approached. They drove to the guesthouse in Niya where Nick and Xue stayed before and turned in early. In the morning, they got on the Tarim Highway and headed for Urumqi, stopping at Korla for the night.

It was midafternoon when they drove into Urumqi the next day. Xue directed Nick to his home near the university. "I'm going to spend some time with my family, tomorrow," he said as he pulled his backpack out of the back. "Are you okay with helping Gail do some apartment hunting?"

Nick looked at Gail. "Is that all right with you?"

Gail nodded. "Sure. See you on Monday, Xue." She moved up front beside Nick. "I'm staying at the Sheridan on Xibei Road. Could you drop me off there?"

"Sure, but I thought maybe you would like to see my apartment. There's a wonderful view of the expressway."

"I wouldn't want to miss a view like that," she said, laughing, "but right now, all I want is a shower and a good meal."

"How about if I take you to your hotel, then come back this evening? I can show you a market where the Uyghurs go. There's a restaurant there with good food and entertainment."

"Deal," she said.

Two hours later they strolled along Qiantang Jiang Lu in a place known as the Wuyi Star Night Market. It was smaller than the Erdao Qiao, but had many venders catering to Uyghur tastes. The street was lit by thousands of hanging lights, and at the far end was a restaurant called Joyous Taste. They sat down at an empty table near the front window. In the back were two Uyghur dancers spinning to lively dotar music.

"You're wearing the necklace I gave you," Nick said, smiling.

"I love it." She pointed to a dish on the menu called Pollo. "What's this? Chicken?"

"That's really good, but actually it's lamb and pilaf with carrots and onions."

"That's what I'm having."

Nick held up two fingers to the waiter passing by. "Pollo."

"I wonder how Michael is making out with the MRI's. At least we don't have to worry about Mohr's budget," said Gail.

"I'm off the hook this time." He looked out the window sadly. "I'm not sure I want to know the results. Guess we'll know Monday or Tuesday."

She studied his face. "What's wrong?"

The waiter returned to their table and set down some nan bread sprinkled with sesame. Nick smiled at Gail mysteriously. "There's something different about Tok Ma."

"Your buddy from the tomb?"

He looked her in the eye. "I'll bet you anything he has twenty-five ribs."

"Like he's your granddaddy one hundred fifty times removed or something?"

"You're very warm – actually, scalding hot. We're more than just related."

Gail burst out laughing. "I get it. You're his reincarnation. No bet. You look too much alike. Wait, on second thought, he's better looking."

"Okay. You asked for it. I'll prove to you I'm from Xinjiang." He rose from his seat and pulled her up by the hand. "Come on, let's go."

"I can't dance to this music," she protested as Nick pulled her to an open space in the back where the couple was dancing.

The diners clapped and nodded in time as he began stepping to the music and raising up his arms. "Let it rip, Gail. Do what they do. We've got to show them foreigners can dance too."

Gail watched how they moved their feet and finally let go of her inhibitions and joined in with Nick. The tempo picked up and the Uyghur couple began twirling. The song continued to pick up speed until it abruptly ended in a quick final chord. The other couple patted Nick and Gail on their backs and helped them keep their balance until the effects of the twirling had worn off.

"Maybe you do have some ancient Xinjiang in you," said Gail when they got back to their table.

"Told you."

"So, what happened out there in the tomb in the desert?"

Nick looked out the window and watched the people strolling by for a moment. "I'm not sure. I had some sort of vision or dream that I traveled back in time to The Lost City. The lake was there, the city, the palace. It was green and real. Michael thinks it was one big hallucination."

"Poor Nick." She held his hand and shook her head. "I don't care what anyone says about you. I'm just glad you're still alive."

"I was in a coma for five days and I think my wiring got rearranged. Sometimes it seems I'm in two places at the same time. Did you know I'm a married man?"

She looked at him quizzically.

"Back in time. I had a wife and two children. Little bits and pieces drift in from time to time." He looked out the window again. "I'm sorry. Forget it."

"I think Michael is right, or else, you spun around too much tonight."

After dinner, they walked about the market place watching the people and enjoying the evening bustle. "I wouldn't mind living around here," said Gail. "How far is it to the museum?"

"Maybe twenty minutes. We're in the Hetian Residential District. It's a good place to live. My apartment is only about three blocks from here."

She stopped and regarded him thoughtfully. "I'd like to see it."

He put his arm around her waist. "We can walk there."

They followed Wuyi Road until they reached the intersection with Hetian Street. "We're here. Would you like the tour?"

Gail nodded.

"This is me," said Nick a minute later, as he opened the door. "It's a bit plain, but it's all I need."

Gail walked over to the front window. "It's a nice view at night. The lights are pretty."

He took her coat and laid it on the couch next to his own.

"What can I get you? Would you like some wine?"

She closed the curtains and faced him. "No thanks."

Nick ran his hand down her side, following the curve of her hips as he pulled her close. He brushed the side of her face with a slow caressing motion and she leaned into his caress. They kissed passionately. Years of scripted behavior fell away as they pressed together tightly, feeling a stronger attraction every moment.

"I don't care if you're married," she said, smiling mischievously. Nick backed away and sat on the couch. She sat down beside him. "I was only trying to be funny. I'm sorry."

"I know. But it doesn't feel funny. I better take you back to your hotel."

Chapter Nine:

Voices Out of Nowhere

ON MONDAYS THE MUSEUM was closed to the public. The down time was used to maintain the exhibits and for administration. Xue was the first to arrive for work and asked Alim to let him into Gail's office. He spread her maps and satellite images over her desk and was still immersed in studying them when she and Nick walked through the door.

"Hi, Xue," said Gail. "You got here early."

He looked up, smiling sheepishly. "Security let me in. I hope you don't mind. My curiosity got the better of me. How did your apartment hunting go?"

"I signed the lease last night. It's near the Wuyi Star Night Market. Easy shopping."

"Sweet. I knew Nick would get you fixed up."

"What do you have going, Xue?" asked Nick.

"I'm wondering how to go about the excavation. If there

are structures two and half meters below the surface, then we need to start with some verticals to see how far down they go."

Nick smoothed over the charts with his hands. "It's not as deep as you think. Most of the structures are only one story, except for the palace. The palace is about five stories tall. We need to start with a focus on the inner grids, doing a horizontal dig. Shovels and buckets, I'm afraid."

"How did you come by this information?" asked Xue.

Nick pointed to the middle of the map. "I'm going by comparisons with the ruins at Cadota in Niya."

Gail looked at Nick, biting her lip. "I ordered ground penetrating radar equipment. I can take a closer look when we return in the spring."

"The GPR is a great idea," said Nick. "Housing tells and the palace at the center grids are of primary interest and we'll be able to know exactly where they are. We can home in on them and save time."

Xue nodded. "And save our backs. But we'll still need a big crew."

A buzzer sounded in the security office and they turned their heads in unison. Alim ran down the hall from security past Xue's office. "What's going on?" asked Gail.

"Someone's at the rear door. Deliveries are being made at the loading dock in the back of the museum," said Xue.

Michael backed through the double doors shouting orders. He locked them open, allowing three coffin sized crates, pushed by handlers, to come through. Nick and the others started down the hall to see what was going on, but Michael motioned them away and directed the handlers to move the crates into the screening room. "I'll meet you in my office in a minute," he said.

A short while later, Michael came bustling in. "I hope you had a chance to relax. We are going to get busy."

"What did you eat for breakfast? A bowl of vitamins?" asked Nick.

"Wise guy," said Michael. "The results from the hospital imaging department are in. I'm going to send you each a link. Pull your chairs over to my desk and I'll show you how to access the system."

Michael explained how the medical imaging system worked and brought up the MRIs of the mummies. The summaries of the two females revealed they were about ages thirteen and thirty, but it wasn't possible to determine their cause of death. For all practical purposes, they seemed healthy. The male was about thirty and had died of a knife wound to the heart from the back.

"What's the matter, Nick?" Michael asked.

Nick bent over, clasping his knees. "I'm not feeling too well."

"You want to take a break?" asked Gail, rubbing his shoulder.

"I'm sorry. I'm all right," he said, forcing himself to straighten up.

After a moment, Gail nodded to Michael and he continued. "Something amazing is that the male had an operation. There is a healed surgical incision in his side. All his organs are intact, but a rib has been removed. Another thing that is odd; this was an extra rib. Some sort of medical anomaly."

"A twenty-fifth rib?" asked Gail.

Nick folded his arms into his chest and began rocking back and forth. "What do you want?" he asked, looking at the ceiling with a dazed expression.

Michael's eyebrows raised. "We're going to come back to this later. Xue, you and Gail can get started writing up the display text for our Shamadù friends. Over in the display room."

Michael closed the medical imaging program. "What's the matter, Nick?" he asked when they were alone.

"Didn't you hear…." He took a deep breath and sat bolt upright, realizing how he must sound to Michael.

"You did the same thing when Ann Lee and I drove you back from the hospital."

"I don't mean to be such a pain."

Michael studied him silently for a moment, then smiled. "I said something that set you off. Maybe it has to do with the coma. You seemed fine up till now, but I think you need to get a checkup."

☙

Nick got an appointment with Dr. Wu in the Department of Neurology at Friendship Hospital for four o'clock that afternoon. He was conducted to the doctor's office and sat in front of his desk for ten minutes. Dr. Wu walked in studying an open chart.

The doctor sat down and looked up from the chart, extending his hand toward Nick. "What brings you here today?"

Nick looked out the window nervously, avoiding eye contact. He had decided only to talk about the accident and the coma, and not to mention the hole in the bone. He gave a quick summary.

"I see that in your chart. How are you feeling now?" asked Dr. Wu.

He regarded the neurologist uneasily. "Well, I hear voices on occasion. Sometimes I get this anxious, nauseated feeling, and kind of seize up."

"Seize up?"

"I feel extremely nervous and clench up … in a ball."

Dr. Wu read the case report half out loud, muttering and nodding his head. "There is a lot in your chart about what happened medically while you were in the coma for five days. Do you remember any of it? Any unusual dreams or experiences?"

Nick squirmed in his seat. "No."

Dr. Wu laughed politely. "You're not alone. It is fairly common for patients who have experienced comas to have vivid dreams or hallucinations. Science can't explain all that goes on in the brain, or what happens to consciousness when everything shuts down."

"It was the most vivid dream I ever had." He took a deep breath and exhaled slowly. "Where should I start?"

"Did you leave your body at any time?" Dr. Wu leaned forward intently.

"Yes. I, ugh, went somewhere else in another body."

The doctor rose and circled the desk. "Cross your leg." He tapped on the kneecap. "The other." He tapped again, then proceeded with a few more basic tests. "Walk across the room for me. Good." He nodded. "Touch your hands behind your back, please. Now follow my pen with your eyes."

Nick was directed to sit down. The last test was to draw a spiral on a piece of paper. Dr. Wu wrote in the chart. "Very good. Before you leave, we will draw some blood for the lab."

"Yes, but doctor, what's wrong with me? Am I crazy?"

"Until the lab gives me the results, I can't give a definite diagnosis, but you're not crazy. Your reflexes and responses look normal. Hallucinations such as voices in the air can happen for a couple of weeks after coming out of a coma, as well as language difficulties or odd behavior. That is not unusual."

Nick gave a sigh of relief. "But the dream?"

Dr. Wu sat down and leaned back. "My guess is a near-death experience: you were unable to breathe and were low on oxygen; you had a wound and lost a lot of blood; it was below zero and the body shut down from hypothermia. You narrowly escaped death and went into a coma: an NDE."

"I wasn't unconscious. I was super conscious. Everything was more real than having this conversation with you right now. Only not in this world."

The neurologist smiled patiently. "Conventional science says consciousness is seated in the brain – here on earth. There can be chemical factors causing hallucinations in comas. One theory says an NDE is a DMT dump: the pineal reacts to a threat to the brain and produces N-dimethyltryptamine which can bring on a psychedelic state. Or there is REM intrusion: natural neurotransmitters like serotonin interact with receptors in the neocortex, producing a vivid dream state. There are other theories."

"But when the brain has shut down, where does consciousness go? It must be outside ourselves. In the chaos of the cosmos," said Nick. He suddenly remembered toking on the hookah. "Could smoking hashish have anything to do with it?"

Dr. Wu shook his head. "It could explain a three-hour psychosis, maybe, but nothing like what you experienced." He rose and extended his hand. "It's disconcerting when these things happen. I would appreciate if you would write down as much as you can remember, then email it to me at this address." He handed Nick his business card. "Don't forget your blood test. The lab's down the hall. Here's the order," he said, handing Nick the script.

ભ

By the time Nick got back to the museum, the mummies had been taken to the mummy wing and placed on display. Michael and most of the staff had already gone home and Xue was the only one there. He was finishing up the alternate English scripts to use for the display signs for the Shamadù mummies when Nick found him.

"How did it go at the doctor's?" asked Xue.

"Well... he said I may have had a near-death experience and sometimes there can be some after effects. Like hallucinations. They're supposed to be gone in a week or so."

"No brain worms?"

Nick laughed. "None."

"I bet that's a relief. I would have thought they would find a couple." He gathered the scripts he had written and handed them to Nick. "Can you proofread my English for me?"

Nick nodded while reading them over. "Very good," he said, handing them back.

"I'll give them to the display department tomorrow. I'm going to call it a day. See you."

"I'm leaving in a minute or two myself. See you," said Nick. He returned to his office and filed away the papers on his desk, then turned off the lights. Other than the night guards, he was the last one in the museum. Nick made his way to the mummy wing and stopped to check on his ancient family. The lighting had been lowered to night mode and cast an eerie light over the exhibits. He looked down at the desiccated remains of his wife and daughter.

"I failed you," he whispered quietly beneath his breath, "but I haven't forgotten." He moved over to Tok Ma and studied the reclining form in silence. After a moment, he slid the glass top to one side and pulled back Tok Ma's coat to expose the leather pouch that contained the magic bone. Nick opened the pouch, still supple after 3,800 years, and removed the bone.

"Nicholas," said a voice from nowhere. "Do not forget."

"I remember, Fenhuang," he replied. Nick looked up at a surveillance camera in the ceiling when a detector chirped. He put back the bone, smoothed the coat into place, then slid the top back.

Chapter Ten:

Lunatic Awakening

VISITATION TO THE MUSEUM usually declined in the winter, but the Chinese 13th National Winter Games of 2016 were held in Urumqi that year and brought in a surge of winter tourists. Although the games ended January 30th, the popularity of the event, held in the brand-new sports arena set in the backdrop of the Heavenly Mountains, did much to dispel Xinijang's image of social unrest.

Gail, Xue, and Nick, spent much of the winter planning the excavation of The Lost City and spent hours every day preparing a topographical map of the site with various survey points that would help them establish settlement patterns and develop a theory about where the people used to live and why they had settled there. Gail worked on a strategy involving the use of nondestructive techniques such as magnetometers and electrical resistivity meters to locate artifacts and structures without digging. Xue was an excellent cartographer and updated the map constantly. The plan to accomplish their goals evolved continually.

Michael worked at procuring the resources they required: trailers, tents and walkie-talkies, three Unimogs, forty diggers, forty shovels and picks, four dozen rolls of twine, six Nikons, and hand trowels. The list kept growing.

After the archaeological team had been brainstorming all morning, Nick walked into Michael's office and sat down by his desk. "We need a bulldozer. A big Cat."

"A bulldozer?"

Nick nodded. "A big one. Like for digging foundations."

"This is not that kind of excavation, Nick," said Michael. "We're going to shovel and sift."

Nick sucked in a lungful of air, letting it out slowly. "I understand the importance of thoroughness, but there's too much to dig in less than twenty years. We need to go straight to the palace and the king's burial chamber first. Not just to have something for the tourists, but to save time and money. The funding may not last forever. I know where the good stuff is and how deep to go. Why spend years sifting dead sand when we can do it in less than one?"

Michael's eyebrows met in the middle. "We have to proceed with caution and document everything with care. There are others wanting to know the proper procedures have been followed. We can't take shortcuts because you have a hunch." He crossed his arms and huffed with exasperation.

"It's like trying to talk to a pile of rocks." Nick stormed out of the room and steamed down the hallway.

Michael went to Xue's office where Gail and Xue worked over the map. "What's wrong with that guy?" he asked. "What a goddamned hothead!"

"The bulldozer, you mean?" Xue shook his head. "I don't know what his rush is. He seems to go off from time to time."

The mummy wing was empty of visitors when Nick got there. He stood by Lu An's case and looked down silently. The room melted away and he stood beside her at the lake, holding her hand. The air was clean smelling and the lake glistened like a thousand mirrors. "I'm sorry. I'm doing the best I can." He became aware that someone was standing next to him.

"Mr. Taylor?" asked a man dressed in a well-tailored suit and wearing a camel-haired coat. He tipped his hat. Nick stared at him as the image of the past faded away. "Mr. Nicholas Taylor?" the man asked again.

"I'm sorry. What can I do for you?" Nick said.

"My name is Henryk Krauser. I'm a professor with the Leiden Centre for the Humanities, Language, and Culture in Berlin."

"The Leiden Center for Linguistics?" asked Nick. He stuck out his hand. "I'm pleased to meet you."

The professor produced a card from a coat pocket. "I recognized you from your interview on TV. I'm giving a lecture at the University of Xinjiang next week and wanted to talk to you. The lecture is called 'Tracking the Tocharians: Their History and Genetics'. I have some questions about the tomb. Perhaps we can talk."

Nick glanced at the card and smiled. "I'd be delighted to, professor. I'm not knowledgeable about the language, I'm afraid."

"Don't worry about that. It's not as difficult as you might think." Henryk pointed to the coffin containing Tok Ma's daughter. "Tu chacar." He pointed down at Lu An before them. "Tu säm." Gliding lightly to Tok Ma, he peered down into the case. "Pacar." Henryk looked up at Nick and gestured at him with a bony hand covered by translucent skin, smiling strangely. "Tu." He nodded and repeated: "tu."

Nick could barely swallow. "That's more than a language lesson, professor."

"Paterfamilias," he replied, still smiling. "It's not that hard to learn. Why don't we get together tomorrow at the university? I can show you some good books on Tocharian. Perhaps we could visit Bezeklik at some point? I know of some caves that are not open to the public. You would find them interesting."

ↅ

Nick met Henryk Krauser the following morning at an apartment used for professors in residence on the edge of Xinjiang University campus. The professor answered the door dressed in an Austrian walking suit and mountain hat.

"You may want to wear something a little warmer. It's about -12 Celsius," Nick cautioned.

"I'm fine. This is for you," he said, shoving a book into Nick's hands. He had written on the title page of *Ancient Tocharian* with an elaborate flourish: *To Nick. Best wishes to a fellow time traveler – Henryk Krauser.*

Nick thumbed through the book. "Thank you. It will take some time to assimilate this."

"You may not be aware of it, but it is commonly believed there are two Tocharian dialects: A and B. Bezeklik is 'B', a later form written around the time of the Buddha. 'A' goes back about three thousand years. My book focuses on writings before that from five thousand years ago."

Nick shook his head in disbelief. "Wow. That's a long time for anything to last."

"The Bezeklik ones didn't last very long. Albert von Le Coq brought the scrolls from the caves at Bezeklik back to Berlin in the 1920s, but those originals were destroyed by Allied bombing in the war. Luckily, there were some copies. New caves were found that contained much older scripts on tablets of wood, but they were kept secret to prevent further culture theft. Because they had been sealed with no humidity or light, there was little deterioration. They are collections of legends dating back over five thousand years ago. I have photos of them in my office that I want to show you."

They walked briskly for two blocks to the humanities building where Henryk had an office. He motioned Nick to have a seat as he pulled a dossier from the bookshelf and laid out several large prints on a table. They were of tablets of hand brushed Tocharian text. Henryk turned on a desk lamp and watched intently as Nick bent over them.

"A bit like Sanskrit, but I can't make out anything," said Nick.

"It's proto Indo-European. Did you find any writings in the tomb?"

"No. As a matter of fact, we are hearing claims that the mummies aren't even Tocharian, but every other ethnic group under the sun, because no writings have been found."

Henryk gesticulated matter of factly. "Tocharians tended to assimilate with other cultural groups in their wanderings, and if they did keep records, they were usually mercantile in nature. Often there are no writings, except in places like Beze-klik, where there were priests."

"There are the tattoos. What do you make of them?'

"They are spells for safe crossing to the afterlife." Nick noticed Henryk's hands were shaking. "I want to ask you," said Henryk; "Did you find trinkets or talismans in the tomb?"

Nick shook his head. "There were piles of clothing. Some blankets. Bracelets and earrings."

"No little statues, or oracle bones? A magic pouch?" Henryk was staring intently.

Krauser's eye ticked. Nick sensed the man was driven by an overwhelming need of some kind. He shook his head. "None."

"Haa!" Krauser held up a print and read in a guttural voice. "Toy vicanmasa sivenäse pile näsait yamasäle. Ney śarām. Yam-c ñakta śaranne astan eske mrestiweśc. Yam śarāmne po śaulanmasa. Ayo astāmts, saim lkāssämtarne täntsi lyauto yukāntassem pwāra rämt. Let me translate for you: by these magical skills, a wound to the raphé of the people. A spell is to be cast by the evil king and he will take them into his bones, even unto his skull, so they may serve him."

Nick's mouth fell open and he stared wide eyed. Henryk Krauser continued. "One shall come who has many lives, and he shall be the people's refuge. He will send the evil one through the opening in the bone - yukāntassem - like the yukānta fires." He pointed at Nick. "Tu."

"No one believes that stuff."

"We all choose to believe what we want to believe. It's called free will. Do you have the bone?" He tilted his head spastically to one side and the disks made popping sounds. "I would so love to hold it."

Nick's head began to swim. The characters on the tablets seemed to move and change shape. "It's safe. I have to go. Thank you, professor."

"For what?"

"They thought I was crazy, then they told me it was a hallucination, an NDE, and I started to believe it. Now I know better."

Nick returned to the museum and stopped at the security office. "It's been a while," said Lu Wang, looking up from his desk. "What have you been up to?"

"Brainstorming. We've been pretty busy."

Wang nodded. "Well, the big bucks and all that."

"Yeah. I wanted to ask you about the alarm systems in the mummy wing. What if someone just grabbed something out of the case and ran out the door? What do we have going besides cameras and motion detectors?"

"Why? Are you planning a robbery?" Wang grinned lopsidedly.

Nick laughed. "Not me. But I heard the new thing in natural medicine was crushed mummy fingers. You know how people eat ground up tortoise shell, rhino horn and donkey skin? You never know. Could you put locks on the cases?"

Wang glanced at the security panel containing the museum keys and stroked his chin. "No wonder you get the big bucks. Alim can install them tonight."

"You're a good man."

Nick's next stop was Michael's office. "What?" Michael snapped.

"I'm not here about the bulldozer. I stopped by to tell you about someone I met from Leiden University. He's the world's leading expert on Tocharian and he's giving a lecture on the history of the language next week. I think we all should go. We ought to include an exhibit on the Tocharians here at the museum."

"Who is it?"

"Henryk Krauser."

Michael squinted for a moment. "No. The name doesn't ring a bell, But that's not a bad idea about the exhibit. I'll put you in charge."

"First, I'm learning the language – in my spare time, of course. Look what he gave me." Nick held out Krauser's *Ancient Tocharian*.

"Pretty thick book."

"Lots of pictures." He tucked the book under his arm and turned to go. "I'm sorry I was such a hothead yesterday."

Michael got up and patted Nick on the shoulder. "Me too. I'm not going to rule out the bulldozer."

⁎

In every spare moment during the following weeks, Nick had his head buried in books on the Tocharians and their language. He frequently visited the university library until late at night and often stopped in to visit Henryk Krauser. Nick asked Henryk to read passages of Tocharian and recorded him to learn the enunciation. Of course, not even Henryk knew for sure how it sounded because it hadn't been spoken for over a thousand years. But he spoke it as though he meant it.

The museum archaeological staff attended Henryk's lecture along with other academics. The auditorium was nearly half full and Henryk remarked happily afterward it was the largest audience he had ever had.

As the weather began to warm and the snow began to melt, Nick had a large display installed in the mummy wing next to the Shamadù mummies. He filled it with reproductions of Henryk's cave prints and installed an audio system that played clips of Henryk reading the text when a button was pushed. Pictures of Tocharian settlements in the Tarim basin were included.

"It's excellent," the professor commented when it was finished. He pressed the play button and smiled at the sound of his voice.

"Tusa śpālmem plāskam seme-sseme kärtsauñe," said Nick. "You have done a good deed. Thank you, professor."

"You see, it's not that difficult. My pleasure. So, maybe we could go to see those caves now?"

Nick sighed. "I wish I could, but we're leaving for Shamadù tomorrow to begin the excavation. I'm not sure when we'll be back."

"Oh. Well then, perhaps you could show me the shaman's bone before you go. I think I have earned it." He frowned at the lock on the case.

"I can't. Sorry, professor."

Chapter Eleven:

The Funerary Chamber

"LET'S GO IN HERE," said Xue, watching the GPS coordinates instead of the road. They were about 8 km south of the town of Shamadù on a barren stretch of Highway 315. The desert was level with the shoulder of the road and the Unimog made the transition from road to sand seamlessly.

Nick stopped the vehicle and climbed down to scan the horizon with binoculars. "This looks good. Should be more direct going in here than through the town."

Xue pulled a pole and a hammer out of the vehicle's back storage compartment and drove it into the ground close to the shoulder of the highway, then tied on a flag that read EXCAVATION. They proceeded to drive across the desert, stopping every hundred meters to put up a marker flag until they came to a spot about five hundred meters east of the yardang near the tomb. The temperature had warmed considerably during the day and the river in the distance had started flowing again as the snow in the Kunlun melted to feed it. A strong wind blew sand into their eyes as they set up tents and stowed the gear they had brought along.

They cooked their dinner quickly and ate inside their tent as the wind buffeted the sides. Xue and Nick unfolded the grid map and made their plans for organizing the others as they began arriving over the next few days. There weren't many dunes in the place they had picked, so the camp would be easy to set up and they would have a clear path to the excavation site.

Michael and Xue believed the summer months would be too hot to work and would require that they take a hiatus from the dig until fall. Nick and Gail favored scaling down to a skeleton crew in the summer months and working at night with floodlights. Nick argued that the proximity of the town and the influx of resources into southern Xinjiang made it possible to move more quickly than in the past. They could bring in an airconditioned trailer to sleep in during the day and keep the dig going at night.

Xue and Nick staked string gridlines over the areas where the palace and the back streets of The Lost City were thought to lie. Two days later, Gail, Michael, and ten workers from the university arrived. Nick helped Michael and Gail unload a hand powered ground penetrating radar device from a flatbed Unimog. The radar device was the size of a lawn mower and sat on four wheels. Gail snapped a digital panel onto the handle.

"Aren't there more workers coming?" he asked.

"We got you covered; fifteen more," she replied.

Michael smiled reassuringly. "Don't worry. I hired Jih-Wen Chang and his crew. They'll be here next week after we do some testing and get everything laid out."

After additional tents were set up, Nick walked them out to the gridlines he and Xue had staked. "Where do you want to start, Gail?" Michael asked.

Gail pointed to the rectangles of string in the middle. "I'll start there and work outward."

"Excellent," said Nick. "That's over Xie Pu's court."

Michael huffed. "After the imaging, we dig test pits."

"No need. I've made it easy for you. There's a five-story palace with a throne down there. Wait till you see what comes up on the GPR screen. Bring in the diggers."

"One thing at a time," said Michael, starting back toward the camp.

Gail hooked her arm in Nick's. "I believe you."

The image scanning proved Nick to be right. The lack of moisture in the ground allowed for deeper penetration by the GPR and produced higher resolution images than normal. A large wooden structure surrounded by still upright palisades was revealed in the pictures. The images were stored on a SIMMS chip and taken back to the camp to be reviewed by Michael.

"Okay, we start digging," he said with a smile. "Set up the sifters. And lots of photos of everything, no matter how insignificant it seems. Log everything." Michael turned to Nick. "Good going, Nick."

ぐろ

Jih-Wen Chang and his team of local laborers showed up with their own wheelbarrows and the pace of digging increased dramatically. The spoil, however, didn't give up any artifacts as it passed through the sifting screens. At the end of the first week, a plough was attached to one of the Unimogs and the pile of filtered sand pushed away into a mound. The plough wasn't the bulldozer Nick had hoped for, but it sufficed.

It was on Monday, when the museum was closed and Nick had just returned from the dig, that Michael summoned him to his tent. He was in a Skype session on his laptop with Lu Wang. Standing next to Wang was Henryk Krauser. Michael turned the laptop sideways so Nick could see the screen.

"Hello, Nick," said Wang. "This fellow says his name is Dr. Krauser from the university and I should talk to you. We have him on camera trying to pick the lock on one of the cases in the mummy wing. Do you know him?" Wang pushed Henryk in front of the lens.

"I told him I needed to check something on the exhibit, but when you weren't there I tried to open it myself without bothering anyone. Tell him I am working with you, Nick," said the angry academic.

"I know him well. We worked on the Tocharian exhibit together. Was anything taken from the case, Wang?"

"No. He couldn't pick the lock."

"Why didn't you ask us to have the case opened for you, Henryk?" asked Michael.

"Like I said, I didn't want to bother anyone."

Nick looked at Michael and shrugged. "Let's let him go. No harm was done."

"Let him go, Wang," said Michael. "But Henryk, you'll have to wait until I get back in a few days. Come see me then. It's museum policy that I be there with you, okay?" He ended the Skype session. "Krauser is an odd fellow, don't you think?"

⁂

Michael's duties at the museum called him back to Urumqi on Wednesday. He informed the team that he had placed Nick in charge. The excavation continued its pattern of digging and sifting. After the first few weeks had passed the days grew noticeably hotter. Chang complained to Nick his men were becoming exhausted and needed to rest during the hottest part of the day. It was decided to work from sunrise to eleven in the morning and from three in the afternoon until sundown. They put reflective tarps over their tents, but that made only a slight improvement. Nick picked up box fans from the hardware store in town and ran them off a generator, but they were not much more effective than trying to cool off with a hair dryer.

He wanted to bring in an airconditioned trailer, but Chang convinced him it would be too difficult to pull it over the sand. It began to look like they might not be able to keep things going past early June and would have to return in the fall.

The next day, when Nick and Gail drove up Highway 315 to go into town for supplies, he noticed a yurt out in one of the fields. "That's it! Look."

Gail stopped the truck and pulled out a pair of binoculars from the glove compartment. A panel with an air conditioner had been fitted into the yurt's circumference. "Problem solved," said Gail, smiling. They placed orders for several yurts with panels and air conditioners when they got into town.

Now that the cooling problem was solved, the work could be extended much longer. As the spring turned to summer, there was a concern that no artifacts of any sort had been found. As the archaeology team sat in the new mess yurt with AC, they talked over a different strategy to move things along faster.

"In Peru at Chan Chan we had a back hoe and front-end loader," said Nick. "Or maybe we could rent a back hoe from someone in town."

No one liked his idea, so he kept it under his hat for the future. A day and half later, Chang called in on Nick's walkie-talkie. "We found something. We're down about four meters and there's the top of a wall."

"Stop everything. We're coming," said Nick.

Xue and Nick piled in a Unimog and sped to one of the

front grids where Gail and Chang were troweling around the top of a section of palace wall. The work crew was yelling in Uyghur as Nick jumped out and ran to take a look. "This is what we came here for," he shouted ecstatically.

Gail squeezed him in a hug. "We're in the right place."

Chang wore a happy grin. He stood and shook Nick's hand. "Congratulations, Mr. Taylor. The Lost City has been found."

One of the workers who had been shoveling about fifteen feet away shouted and pointed down to a wooden bracket. Xue took a camera out of the truck and snapped photos. Xue identified the artifact. "A dougong. A roof support."

"Okay, everybody," said Nick, holding up his hands in the air. "We're going to go back to the camp now. Chang, bring the whole crew. We now have a find. Let's have a little celebration, rest a bit, then talk about what comes next."

The camp's main yurt served as both a mess hall and a meeting place. Although it was early for lunch, the camp cook fired up the stove and began setting out a buffet of lamb filled samsas and hummus. Nick went to the refrigerator and brought out several beers for the museum team. He motioned to Chang to join them at their table.

"Care for a cold one?" asked Nick, holding out a beer.

Chang took the bottle and had several deep swigs. "Should I offer the men some?" Nick asked.

"No. They don't drink," said Chang. "But, I do."

Nick clinked his bottle to Chang's. "I want to thank you and your crew for the great job you have done. You guys are good. Have you done this before?"

Chang smiled wryly. "Over at Niya. I know these men, that's why I picked them. They are professionals."

Gail and Xue set their food on the table and sat down. Gail grabbed a beer and twisted off the top. "So, we found a building..."

"Palace," Nick corrected.

"Let's say it is the palace," said Gail. "The problem is, are we at the roof and have to go down five stories, or has it collapsed like what usually happens and we are at ground level looking at a pile of rubble? The images don't show all that."

Everyone grew quiet. Xue watched them thinking with solemn looks on their faces. "Why is everybody looking so serious? This is the time to celebrate."

"It is serious. Do we have to dig for five years, or twenty-five?" asked Nick. He looked at Chang. "The palace – it's a palace - covers about eighteen grids. How long do you think it will take to unearth eighteen grids going down four meters?"

Chang chewed on a mouthful of samsa, bobbing his head as he calculated. "It's hard to say for sure, but maybe by early November. The spoil is mostly grit, but we don't know yet what it contains."

After they had finished eating, Nick pushed their plates and empty beer bottles to one end of the table. "Xue, spread out the map, will you?" he asked. Chang pulled a pack of Camels out of his shirt pocket and lit one.

"That will stunt your growth, kid," said Xue as he unfolded the grid map on the table. He made a face and fanned the air.

Chang broke the cigarette in half and dropped the burning portion in an empty beer bottle where it sizzled out. "Sorry," he said. He rose and stood by Xue, staring down intently at the map. "What's this?" He tapped on a point at the base of the Kunlun.

"All right, genius," said Xue, "explain everything so we all are on the same page."

Nick leaned across the table and pointed to the grids covering the thin white outline of the palace. "This is where we are today." He moved his finger north of where the palace lay. "This circular outline over here – it's about a kilometer and a half from the palace – is the city burial mound."

Nick felt his heart racing and had to clear his throat several times.

"Are you okay?" asked Gail, patting him on the back.

"I'm just getting a little choked up thinking about it, that's all." He took a deep breath and a gulp from the bottle. "Between the mound and the palace is the actual Lost City of Shamadù. It's about twice the size of Bezeklik. We're going to need a lot more help."

He put down his beer and pointed to a small rectangle near the palace. "This structure is about forty meters from the palace. It's a funerary building where religious rites took place.

Inside is the entrance to a tunnel." He slid his finger along the map to the base of the mountain. "To answer your question, Chang, the tunnel leads to an ancient king's burial chamber. Here, beneath the mountain. The spoils of his kingdom are in there, along with those who serve him in the afterlife."

Chang's eyes widened. "How do you know this?"

"He has a hunch," said Xue.

Nick grinned sardonically. "Täntsi lyauto yukāntassem."

"Krauser told you this?" asked Xue, scowling. "Can you give us some scientific basis for this?"

"No. You'll just have to trust me."

They regarded Nick with raised eyebrows.

"He's been right about everything so far," Gail retorted.

Nick stood up and looked around the table. "We are on the cusp of something bigger than all of us. No matter what lies beneath the surface, there is a lifetime of work before us. Michael is going to Beijing next week to speak with the Institute of Archaeology and the Cultural Heritage Institute which were instrumental in the excavations at the Niya site. I'm sure he can get us the help we need, but it will take months to get approval."

"We don't have much time left. Soon it will be fall," said Chang. "Counting the students, there are only thirty-five in our crew."

"That's right, Chang. I think we should concentrate on the tunnel and get to the burial chamber first. That will draw the most attention and get us more resources for our work."

Xue shook his head. "Save the best for last. The First Emperor Qin's's burial chamber has never been opened after forty years of excavation. It can wait. Concentrate on what we have so far."

Nick turned to Gail. "Do you agree?"

"This isn't the funerary city of Qin Shi Huang Di," said Gail. "I agree with you, but for another reason entirely. There is looting all over the planet every day. We better get there first before someone else does."

"That is an excellent point." Nick looked at Chang. "How long can your men work? The middle of November?"

Chang spun his empty bottle nervously, then shrugged. "I'll ask the men, but they've been away from their families for a long time. Maybe the first week of November. After that it's too cold anyway."

"I understand. We'll have to halt for the cold months, but I'll need you in the spring again."

"Yes. Without a doubt, we will be back in the spring."

"Good. We'll finish out this week digging test shafts around the palace wall to get some samples to take back. Then start on the tunnel full time."

Chapter Twelve:

Execration

"THIS IS A GUI vessel," said Xue. The buff colored pottery had been unearthed in the second of the three shafts in the palace area and was still partially covered in places by a thin shell of black lacquer. It stood balanced on three hollow tapering legs supporting a cylindrical body that widened toward the rim. Xue set down a flared lacquered wooden goblet next to it. "These two pieces are part of a three-piece gu set used in a libation ritual for someone of high status. If only we had the jiao pottery vessel that is missing. There is only one complete gu set known to be in existence."

"We found these in the third shaft," said Chang. He handed Xue a photo and log sheet and motioned to a worker to bring over a basket containing an intricately carved jade hair pin and a jade bracelet with monster faces carved upon it.

"Ahh," said Xue reverently. He arranged them in the shade

beneath the awning on a work table. "What do you say, Nick? Widen the shaft a meter or two? We are on to something."

Nick shook his head slowly. "It's so hit or miss. We have plenty enough right here to satisfy the Institute of Archaeology. Let's get it all documented and send the report to Michael tonight. Tomorrow we'll begin on the tunnel to the tomb."

"Come on, man. The jiao is probably a few feet away. What's another day or two of digging?"

"You heard Michael. Three exploration shafts, then the tunnel."

Chang looked from Xue to Nick and shrugged.

"Tomorrow the tunnel," said Nick emphatically.

More objects were uncovered in the third shaft by the end of the day. Not widening the shaft didn't preclude going deeper. The new discoveries included a stone chime and a studded brass bell that played three different notes depending on where it was struck. When Michael received Xue's transmission of the artifacts they had found, he instructed him to store them in boxes in the supply tent until museum handlers could be sent down to crate them and bring them back to Urumqi. He would take the photos and documentation Xue sent with him on his trip to The Institute of Archaeology in Beijing.

Early the next morning, Nick stood with Chang by the grids that marked where the funerary chamber and entrance to the tunnel to the king's tomb were buried. Chang cupped his hands around a lit match and bent his head to light a cigarette. In that moment, Nick looked to the top of the Kunlun and saw the apparition of a great bird with flaming plumes perched on top. Nick jabbed Chang with his elbow.

"What?" said Chang, taking a deep drag.

Nick pointed to the mountain top, but Fenghuang was gone. "Nothing. It must have been the sun." He unfolded the map and checked the grids again. "Have the screens moved here."

"The soil's loser, too. We can dig pretty fast here."

"Good. Put in two additional screens using the large mesh. We need to speed things up. I want to make it to the base of the mountain before we break camp in November."

Chang blew out a cloud of smoke and smiled. "I'm with you, boss."

The two men walked back to the mess as everyone was finishing their breakfast. Nick outlined the new course of action. Jih-Wen Chang directed his men to move the screens, and by late morning, the full excavation of the ritual chamber and tunnel entrance was underway.

The soil above the chamber was mostly sand and was not as deep as they had originally thought. By afternoon of the following day, the top of the tile roof was discovered, then progress on the unearthing slowed dramatically. Chang realized from there on down, the entire structure had been buried in a mix of earth, sand, and clay brought in from somewhere else and packed so tightly that it was nearly as hard as concrete. He brought Nick and Gail over to get their opinions.

Chang tapped on the ground with his trowel. "There goes easy street."

"They didn't want anyone getting in. Even a bulldozer couldn't budge this," said Gail.

Nick borrowed a shovel from one of the diggers and jumped on the blade to drive it in. There was no penetration. "It's rammed earth. A jackhammer ought to break it up. We only need to dig out this side. Could you get a detailed image of the area with a scan from the side, Gail? We need to know exactly where the entrance lies."

"Sure. I can do that." She untied her neckerchief and shook out the dust.

Nick folded his arms and ground the toe of his boot in the tamped dirt. "I'm guessing, but it might take another week or two to get inside. Somehow, we'll have to get hold of some jackhammers." He looked at Chang. "Any ideas?"

Chang's eyes lit with wry amusement. "Am I not Jih-Wen Chang? I have a friend in Niya. How many do we need?"

"Gimme some skin, Chang." Nick raised his palm in the air and Chang tilted his head in bewilderment. "Show him, Gail." He and Gail smacked their palms together. "It's American for 'way to go.'"

"Way to go?" asked Chang, returning Nick's high five.

"It means we're team players. Anyway, three jackhammers will be enough."

"I'll have them here tomorrow afternoon."

❧

The concrete busters did a good job in breaking apart the blocks of rammed earth that had been laid around the ritual building as a barrier to entry. Most of the blocks were removed intact, numbered, and stored nearby in stacks. Before the week was out, the massive doors that had sealed the ritual chamber for millennia were exposed.

The team stood watching as Xue dusted off hieroglyph-like symbols that had been etched in relief on a brass plaque embedded on the door. "What does it say, Xue?" asked Nick.

Xue exhaled slowly and scratched his head. "These are pictographs from the Neolithic Period before there was formal writing. I don't know. We need to send photos to Michael."

"It's a curse," said Chang. "I've seen them before. The priests put them there to scare away those who believe." Chang laughed. "I'm still here."

"Can you make an entry in the journal, 'execration text,' and send the photo to Michael?" Nick handed a camera to Xue.

They were more at a loss, however, as to how to gain entrance to the interior. The ancient timbers of the door were bound in brass and hung from the inside without handles or a mechanism with which they could be opened from the outside. The exterior walls were made of half ton masonry blocks and were without windows. A debate ensued that lasted into the evening. Disassembling parts of the roof or removing wall blocks was discussed, but they were reluctant to cause damage to the ancient structure. Chang had listened politely without saying a word.

"We're not getting anywhere, let's call it a day and sleep on it," said Nick.

"There may be a way."

"How, Chang?" asked Nick.

"I worked at a dig once, where a door like this was opened with levers. We attached a beam across the bottom of the door, then placed levers under the beam and raised it until high enough to slip under. Very little damage was done."

"But wasn't it locked in some way on the inside?"

"The gate was sitting in stone channels and held down by weights on the inside. We used posts and levers to raise it."

"Skin, Chang. We'll get started on the gate first thing in the morning."

Chang high fived and smiled happily.

"We better put on a guard now that we know how easy it is," said Gail.

Nick nodded. "I'll ask Michael if he can hire some more security people tomorrow."

"This part of Xinjiang has a certain reputation," said Xue. "It will be better to start tonight."

"I'll stand watch. It was my idea," said Gail.

Nick looked from one face to another. "Do you all know how to use a firearm? I've got a revolver for emergencies."

Chang raised his arm and flicked his cigarette away, then shook his head.

Xue let out a laugh. "I can use a bullwhip."

"Gail?" asked Nick.

"I'm better at screaming."

"What a bunch of smartasses. Give me your matches, Chang," said Nick. He broke four matches into different lengths and each took one. They held them out and compared. "Gail, you're first watch. I'm second. Xue, you're third. Chang, fourth. There's an airhorn in the supply tent you all can share. If there's trouble, just sound the horn for help. Let's get back for diner."

Gail ate quickly, then went to the supply tent to pick up some things for guard duty. She made her way to the funerary chamber entrance carrying a canvas camping chair and a portable propane heater. After unfolding the chair, she ignited the heater and began warming her hands. Temperatures had been freezing at night as fall drew closer. The sky was clear and the stars were bright against the dark outline of the building. In back of her were rammed earth blocks which prevented a clear view of the camp. There was the sound of pots banging in the mess tent and some arguing in the distance, then silence. A few minutes later, she leaned back in her chair and picked up a book and began reading by flashlight. After a couple of chapters she thought she heard a ringing sound and looked in the direction of the blocks. She put down her book and picked up the air horn.

"It's me," said Nick, emerging from behind the dark shapes carrying a cup of coffee and stirring it with a spoon.

"Good thing I don't have a gun. I might have shot you."

"I'm inclined to agree with you." Nick held out the cup. "Like some? I have a thermos of coffee and some trail bars in my bag."

Gail stood, then stamped her feet and took the cup. "I'm freezing, thanks."

Nick reached into his bag and pulled out the thermos and a tin cup. "Guess it was pretty boring."

"I like the quiet of the desert at night."

He looked up at the stars hanging over the horizon. "It doesn't get any better, does it?"

"Well, it could be a little better."

He poured himself some coffee. "How's that?"

Gail took a deep breath. "You've been a stranger since we came out here to the dig."

"What do you mean by 'stranger'? We see each other every day."

"We've been kind of … drifting away … from one another. I thought …"

Nick looked into her eyes with a faraway look. "I don't mean to be. It's just that, back at the museum, I was having some personal difficulties and I didn't want to drag you into them."

"You ought to talk about it. Don't hide it."

Nick bit his lip and turned away. "Before, when I was acting kind of strange and hearing things back in Urumqi, I felt like a bit of a … freak. People are still thinking, down underneath it all, that I'm crazy. You don't want to get mixed up with me."

Gail put down her coffee and took his hand. "If most people went through what you did, they'd be dead, or at least out of their minds. Don't feel that way. We wouldn't be here doing what we are doing now if it wasn't for you. You've been right all along. All your crazy hunches. You've got something nobody else has."

"What?"

Gail searched his face, groping for the words. "I don't know exactly. Some kind of insight. You're a genius of some kind."

Nick let out a deep sigh. "That's just it. I don't just feel like I'm uncovering the past. I feel like I'm going home. Things come through in little pieces at a time, like déjà vu, but I know I was here a long time ago. I'm going back to where I belong."

"Like, get-back-in-time belong?"

Nick nodded. "Yeah."

She released his hand and stepped back. "We all live in the house that Jack built."

Nick stepped closer and took her in his arms. "No matter what happens, I want you to know, I couldn't make it without you. I love you."

"Oh, God. Promise me you'll go back to see that neurologist when we get back to Urumqi." Gail broke away and spun on her heels to leave.

"Gail."

She stopped and faced him, trying to hold back her tears. Nick held out the book. "Don't forget your book."

☙

The team assembled in the morning at the funerary chamber entrance along with the students and Chang's workers. Nick supervised the measuring and cutting of the beam that would be used to lift the door. Chang put down wooden blocks to rest the beam on as it was attached, then Nick and four workers picked it up and began maneuvering it into position. Gail appeared from behind the rammed earth blocks and watched with folded arms.

Nick turned his head and stopped, causing them to halt. Gail frowned angrily.

"What's the matter?" he asked.

She looked at the men holding the beam, then walked over to Nick. "I don't like being toyed with. Everything you said to me last night was a lie. You could have blown me off a better way than that."

"No, Gail, no. Why would I make it up? I told you the truth because I care about you."

"It was easier to make up that story than tell the truth, you coward."

The men holding the beam began talking among themselves in Uyghur. "Hey, settle it later," said Chang. "We got work to do. That thing's heavy."

Gail spun around and started back to camp. Nick let go of the end of the beam and the men dropped it to the ground. He caught up with her and stood in her way. "It was the truth." He lowered his voice: "I'm crazy, I'm sorry. But don't go. We need you. I need you. Come on, this is the moment we've been waiting for. Come on back."

She searched his face for clues and found none. "Okay," she said reluctantly. "Bastard." They walked together back to the funerary door. Gail pointed at Nick and made a face. "He's nuts," she said. The men laughed, nodding their heads knowingly, although none spoke English.

When the beam was attached, Chang set down more wooden blocks to serve as fulcrums and directed several workers to bring over pikes and pry upward. By adding larger fulcrums as the door rose, they were able to achieve enough height for a man to slip under. Chang placed an eighteen-inch block under each side of the opening and told the crew to back down the door to rest on them.

Xue had been recording the operation with a camera. "I bet Michael wishes he was here. Too bad he couldn't make it."

"He'll come down for the opening of the tomb," said Nick. He turned on a flashlight and got down on his stomach and stuck his head beneath the door.

"What do you see?" asked Gail.

Nick started coughing and quickly stood up. "We're going to need floodlights. I could barely see anything. The air is bad in there. Chang, start up the generator and have some fans brought from the supply tent. Bring the lights and cords, too."

Gail knelt by the opening and sniffed. "It smells like sulfur and turpentine. We can't go in there until it's safe to breathe."

"Let's have a think while they're bringing the equipment," said Nick. He sat down in the shade of the chunks of rammed earth and the others sat next to him. "We need to analyze the air. Any ideas?"

"A snake or ground robot," said Gail.

"They're not easy to come by," said Xue.

Nick's jaw clenched. "That's going to slow things up, but we can try. Xue, let me borrow your phone to call Michael and let him know where we are at. There are more resources in Beijing. It's a good thing he's there."

Xue pulled out his phone and dialed Michael, then handed it to Nick. After Nick explained how they opened the funerary chamber and had encountered possibly hazardous conditions, Michael agreed to ask for a robot, but thought that it would be weeks before the technical personnel and equipment arrived.

"Safety is the first priority. Patience must be exercised," Michael cautioned. "I will let you know in a day or two what I find out."

"I understand," said Nick.

"One more thing. I have a translation of the pictograph Xue sent. It means: If any man enters, the King shall rise and eat his soul. I know how you all feel, but whatever is in there, it has waited thousands of years. A few more weeks won't make any difference."

"Whatever is in there? Do you think there are booby traps?"

"I have no idea, but the fumes are not a good thing. Maybe that is the booby trap. There could be radon, too. Talk to you soon."

"Good bye," said Nick. He handed the phone back to Xue. "I think you all heard what he said."

"That's one spooky execration," said Gail. "I'm for waiting."

Nick stared at the doorway, rubbing his chin. "Michael's the boss. But we'll have to shut down the dig in a few weeks. I think we can aim the floodlights inside and take some photos from the entranceway while we're waiting for an answer." He continued staring at the entrance, rocking back and forth.

Ten minutes later the generator could be heard starting, then Chang emerged from behind the rammed earth blocks uncoiling an extension cord, accompanied by two workers carrying floodlights, tripods, and some box fans.

Nick grabbed a tripod and attached a floodlight, then plugged in the cord and slid the lights under the door and righted the stand. "Let me have the camera, Xue," he said, motioning to Xue impatiently. Nick crouched at the door and panned the camera inside as the others crowded behind him to stare at the viewer.

The chamber gave up its secrets, unseen for thousands of years; vast collections of life-like jade statuary and fantastic terracotta beasts. The light faded into the distance, unable to reach the far end of the interior. In back of the statues were marble arched doorways leading to more rooms. Nick dragged a tripod leg sideways and aimed the light into one of the rooms, revealing marble congs on one side; the other side was cloaked in darkness.

"Look at all those!" cried Gail. "What are they?"

"Congs. Used in libations." Nick tried to maneuver the lights to illumine them better, but without success.

"I'm setting up the fans," said Chang. "We will blow in some fresh air and go in and open the door all the way. There is nothing to be afraid of."

"No!" Xue put his hand on Chang's shoulder to restrain him. "You will poison us all."

Chang pushed his hand away, scowling.

As Nick recorded the chamber his eyes were tearing. His hands began to shake, and Gail took the camera from him. "Let me do it," she said softly.

Nick handed her the camera. "This is what I've lived for. I'm almost home." He pulled himself upright and made his way out to the desert alone.

ↄ⌀

The next morning, Gail found Nick sitting by himself in the mess tent with his head down on the table. She sat down beside him. "You look tired."

Nick smiled wanly. "I am. I edited the video footage and sent it to Michael at five in the morning. That and the watch. I could never be a security guard." He forced himself up straight and cracked his neck. "I can't help but notice we are having a conversation."

"What I said about you yesterday was wrong. Some of the stuff you come out with is pretty hard to swallow, but I think you are sincere when you say it. I'm sorry."

Nick patted her hand. "Friends?"

She nodded. "Friends." An awkward silence ensued. "So, what are all those congs for? Do the monster faces on them have a meaning of some kind?

He opened his laptop and began explaining. "Congs have been turning up all over China for hundreds of years, but no one has been able to figure out what they are used for. But I will tell you how they were used here."

Gail laughed. "If only your brain were as big as your head."

"Ouch. I thought we were friends again."

"I'm listening with a healthy degree of skepticism."

He turned his laptop to face her. An enlarged image of a cong filled the screen. It was a marble column covered in carved faces with monstrous eyes and mouths and the top was a concave bowl with dark stains that ran down the sides of the column. "The bowl was used to collect blood. If we have a lab test run, the dark stains will prove to be human blood. Blood used by priests in a ritual to capture the spirit of a sacrificial victim."

"Please, I haven't had any breakfast yet. That is sickening."

"To us." Nick brought up a photo of the dark side of the room and raised the contrast as far as it would go, then tinted the photo green. The outline of a table and a cong was just barely perceptible. "The victims were slain on tables like this one, and their blood drained into the bowl of the cong. Incantations released the life force of the victim and forced it to do the bidding of the priest: advanced necromancy."

Gail jumped up from her seat. "The coffee's ready. I'm going to grab some oatmeal, too. Want some?"

"Sure."

When she got back, Nick brought up an image of the back of the funerary chamber. The floodlights were beyond their limit of penetration and the quality was very grainy. "I have something for you that is more in accordance with scientific principles." He pointed to a large machine-like object. "What do you suppose that is?"

Gail sipped her coffee, staring intently. "I can't guess."

"It's a bellows. Judging by its size, it must have needed several men to operate it. Why do you think they built a bellows?"

Gail shook her head in bewilderment.

"Because, down in the tunnel, there is crude oil or maybe bitumen leaking in somewhere. That is what we are smelling. Crude oil contains hydrogen sulfide and smells like turpentine and rotten eggs. It could eat our lungs out - if it doesn't explode."

"That makes total sense. There are a lot of oil wells in the region, too. But what tunnel?"

Nick used the contrast and tint technique to reveal the outline of the mouth of a tunnel. "I know it's hard to make out exactly what it is, but this is the mouth of the tunnel that goes to the base of the mountain. To Lord Xie Pu's tomb."

Later that morning, Michael contacted Nick and informed him the robotic exploration equipment would not be available until the spring. The camp would have to close earlier than expected and they would resume the next year with more resources at their disposal. The good news was that the Institute of Archaeology would send them a new technically advanced version of Chinese-designed robotic snake with the capability of analyzing the atmosphere and taking pictures in hostile environments. It would be ideally suited for crawling along tunnels and through toxic liquids.

The funerary chamber was sealed. When the security guards arrived, light and motion sensors were placed on the entry door. After the artifacts that had been collected were boxed up and the tents taken down, Nick arranged for their transport back to Urumqi. Thanking Chang and his men for their services, he paid them and let them go. The next morning, Gail, Xue, and he climbed in their Unimog and began the long drive back to Urumqi.

Chapter Thirteen:

Soul Fragment

IT WAS HARD RETURNING to civilization. Nick had almost forgotten how it felt coming to work squeaky clean after showering
and shaving. It was hard to sit still at a desk and work at the computer. The clean city clothes felt tight and seemed to prevent him
from moving freely. He squirmed in his seat for an hour, trying to
catch up with reports and email, then walked to the break room
for a cup of coffee. Gail and Xue had beaten him to the punch.

"Does everybody love paper work as much as I do?" he asked.

"Why do they say 'paperwork'? It's all ones and zeroes now.
I'm still going to need a week to catch up," said Xue.

Gail smiled sadly. "I'm not gloating, but I did mine as I
went along. No big deal."

"Then how come that's not a happy smile?" asked Nick.

"Because there was an email from John Mohr. I have to go
back to the States. He needs me for a new project."

Nick let out a sigh. "I've been dreading this day would come. What if we said you were indispensable?"

"It was supposed to be for six months. It's been ten."

"I can't believe it's been that long. I'm going to miss you," said Xue.

Gail pushed herself away from the table. "I would stay ten more years if I could."   As she walked down the hallway back to her office, Nick caught up with her. "When is your last day?"

"In four weeks."

"The inevitable has arrived, but …" He struggled to find the right words. "I don't want you to go."

"I tried to talk Mohr out of it. He gave me an extra week."

"That's all? Have dinner with me … and maybe see a show."

"Is this a formal date?"

He thought for a moment, watching her eyes searching his. "Two friends sharing some good times."

"I don't think so." She hugged him and kissed him on the cheek, then hurried down the hall.

Xue caught up to Nick as she disappeared into her office. "Don't push the river, it flows by itself."

Nick turned and smiled. "Thanks, Xue. You're probably right."

"I wish I had better advice, my friend. Somehow it will work out."

"Yeah, sure." They walked on for a few moments until Nick broke the silence. "I need to go to the storage room and check on the crates from the dig. Will you help me take inventory?"

"Okay. I can't imagine where we are going to put everything."

Nick unlocked the door and they walked through the screening area into the storage room where the Shamadù artifacts had been taken until they could be researched and placed in a display. He picked up a clipboard with the list of items brought back from the excavation and ticked them off to Xue who located the respective wooden crates. The Gu partial set and stone chime were missing.

"Maybe the display department has them," said Xue. "Let's talk to He Zeng."

⁊

He Zeng was in charge of museum displays. Nick and Xue race walked to his office and asked if any of the crates had been removed from storage. Zeng said not to his knowledge. The three of them returned to the storage area and checked the codes on the labels and studied the tamper tape. "Better talk to security," said Zeng.

An angry scowl spread across Wang's face. "I received the entire truck load myself. The shipment was brought to storage directly from the excavation by our own driver and witnessed by the museum handler. Let's take another look. They must be there."

The search turned up nothing. "They took the best ones. The most valuable – worth a fortune on the black market. It must be someone at the museum who took them," said Nick.

"They'll make a nice touch on some playboy's shelf to impress their friends," added Zeng, shaking his head in disbelief.

"I will notify the police. This is not an ordinary larceny," said Wang. "Discuss this with no one."

"Perhaps there's a simple explanation," said Xue. "Maybe they are sitting on Michael's desk and he just didn't tell anyone."

Zeng's eyes brightened. "Maybe. Curators can cause a lot of trouble. They think they don't have to follow the rules."

Wang frowned. "Michael has been in Beijing. He won't be back until tomorrow. From here on, I'm disabling the finger print IDs and access to the keys. The storage room will be locked for everyone and they must see Alim or me to be let in." He pressed his finger into the ID sensor on the wall and a drawer popped out. He pulled out a key that opened a four-foot-wide, six-foot-high panel in the wall. Inside were row upon row of keys on pegs, each labelled with alpha numerals. The rows and columns were dotted with red and green LEDs."

"How many keys are there?" asked Nick.

Wang shrugged. "A thousand? And if anyone broke into this box, it would do them no good. They must have this sheet … he pulled out a laminated sheet from his shirt pocket … to decode which key is for each exhibit."

"You better not die, Wang," said Nick.

Michael returned the following afternoon and immediately called a meeting in his office. Before he could begin speaking, Nick blurted out the entire story. "I was supposed to keep it to myself, but I think you all should know about it. Someone at the dig must have communicated with someone here at the museum. There's some kind of collaboration going on."

Michael looked up in supplication. "Yě shì zuì le. You are kidding me, right? What's Wang doing about it?"

"He's working with the police. He said to keep it quiet."

"We can rely on him to find the culprit … or culprits. I hope you are wrong, Nick."

He looked about the room. "Any other news? Let's get back to our meeting. As you all know, we will resume work on the dig in the spring when the robot and technicians are available. In the meantime, we will research the artifacts and ready them for display. Which brings us to the next problem: where to put them. Zeng has pointed out that we have no more room for additional displays here. Fortunately, the Institutes of Archaeology and Chinese Culture have come up with a solution. We have been given government approval to be a State Priority Protected Site and will be fully funded under the Block and Road Project. A new museum will be built at Charbashi that will enclose the tomb of the mummies and house the findings from the excavation. A road will be built to the excavation suitable for tour buses."

After cheers and a round of applause, Xue raised his hand. "That's great news, but it may take several years. Are we going to put everything in storage until then?"

"Excellent question. We are going to put The Lost City and the mummies on a world tour until the museum is completed.

The Bowen Museum in California and the Houston Museum of Natural Science have expressed interest. Also, Gail's favorite museum; The Penn Museum in Philadelphia. And that brings me to the next subject: Gail will be returning to Philadelphia at the end of the month. Her stay has been extended once, already. I'm afraid we reached the limit. Wǒmen huì xiǎng nǐ. We will miss you, Gail."

Gail averted her eyes. "It's been such an honor to work here. I will miss you all, more than I can say."

"Jì mò dǎng yijing. I am lonely, already," said Nick softly, so that she did not hear.

☙

The Urumqi police interviewed the museum staff, a process that took most of the week. There were not any leads or clues. They tried to contact Jih-Wen Chang for questioning, but were unable to locate him. When the inspector in charge of the investigation asked Michael for more information about Chang's behavior at the dig, Michael told him that he had hired him personally and that he had been invaluable to the excavation. The inspector explained that Chang was not a suspect, but he may have inadvertently spoken to the wrong person about the artifacts. They needed to know who he had been in contact with. A week went by and Chang was not located.

As the relics from Shamadù underwent a process of repair and preparation for display, pieces of shattered marble from one of the crates were reassembled. Nick recognized it as the top half of a cong and thought it could be put on display. It appeared to be the same as the other congs in the photograph of the funerary room, but without stains. The information on congs in the museum information center was scant and inadequate, so he made a visit to the University of Urumqi library.

There was no way to substantiate his own theories on the purpose of congs. No authoritative sources were to be found that drew any conclusions as to their use. As he poured over long trails of endnotes and bibliographies leading to nowhere, he realized someone was looking over his shoulder.

"I think we met before." The professor was wearing his Australian mountain suit, looking out of place as usual.

"It's me, Professor. Of course, we met before." Nick reached up and shook his hand.

"In another life, Nick."

Nick's brows furrowed as he studied the professor's face. A vague image of two men wearing conical hats standing by a lake floated momentarily through his mind. "I can't remember where I parked my car, let alone my previous life," said Nick. But Henryk Krauser seemed to be connected to him in some indefinable way. He felt it, rather than knew it. "Which one?" he asked.

Krauser shrugged. "I can't say, exactly. Perhaps in fragments of half remembered dreams. I'm sorry I brought it up."

"I have feelings of deja vue sometimes. I know what you

mean." Bits and pieces of his near-death experience flashed through his mind, but nothing connected. "So, what have you been up to?"

"While you've been out hunting for antiques, I found some of my own at Bezeklik. I want to show you some tablets I've finished translating. Come to my office. I think you will find them … relevant."

"Relevant?"

"One in particular. *The Book of Turu.*"

His curiosity aroused, Nick accompanied the professor across the campus to the humanities building through a heavy snowfall. After shaking the snow off in the hallway, Henryk led Nick to his office and unlocked the door.

"This is it. *The Book of Turu.* The original tablets are still at Bezeklik." Henryk pulled an over-sized book of photographic prints off one of the book shelves and set it on the desk.

Nick opened to the first page. "This looks like the Tree of Life. Is Turu another manifestation of the world tree?"

The professor nodded. "These texts describe it as found on a mountain top called The Crown of Heaven. Today, that is a mountain in the Kunlun range in southern Xinjiang. In Chinese mythology the Kunlun were magical mountains. The further west one traveled, the further the mountains moved, never to be found. The Queen Mother of the West lived in them in a magical, walled garden. A paradise. With Fenghuang."

Nick picked up the magnifying glass lying on the desk and

read aloud slowly from a photo plate of a tablet engraved with the Tree of Life. Beneath the tree were words in proto Tocharian lettering. *The higher in the tree, the greater his powers be.*

The professor gazed down at Nick with a patient smile. "*The Book of Turu* is the story of ancient Tocharian shamans. They were born in the Tree of Life and raised by simurghs: monstrous, intelligent birds who were allies of mankind. The shamans lived many lives, sometimes as a woman, sometimes as a man, descending to earth in different bodies and returning to the tree many times. This is a book of ancient wonders, something I had only dreamed of finding in this lifetime. But as I read it, I realized it was not for the first time, and I began remembering. Do you remember me now? It's something you feel, not that you know. Empty your mind."

Something was crawling inside his spine. The room began to spin and he was falling down the sinkhole he had dreamed as a boy. The descent seemed to be for an eternity, when suddenly, instead of hitting the bottom, he came out on the other side of it. Gon Ea and Lu An were running, and he had fallen to his knees at the foot of Lord Xie Pu with a dagger through his heart. He gasped for air and staggered to his feet, panting like a dog.

"It's a lot to take in," said Henryk. "Now do you remember?"

"I think so, although you don't look physically the same." Every nerve in his body was tingling. Each breath like an explosion of energy. Everything looked different.

Henryk patted him on the shoulder. "The body is merely

a convenience. Certainly, this old carcass of mine has outlived its usefulness. At first, I thought I would gain possession of the magic bone and find another life in a different world. But that was before I found the book and understood how selfish that would be. You and I come from the tree, Turu, and have a higher purpose. The magic bone is for you alone so that you may complete your mission."

"It makes sense, in a way. My compulsion to get to the tomb. The feeling that I belong to that distant time, and not in today's world."

"Trust your feelings and intuition. Your gift of insight has not been completely forgotten. I'm giving you *The Book of Turu*. Learn it. It has all the knowledge you need to defeat Lord Xie Pu and free the souls he has stolen."

The professor picked up the book and wrapped it in an oil-skin. He held it out to Nick. "Take it, there is not much time left. A storm has been brewing for 3,800 years and is about to descend upon us."

❧

It was still snowing as he made his way back to his apartment. The sun had set an hour before, but the city was bright with reflected light and the air itself glowing with snowflakes. Nick unwrapped the book and began reading as soon as he got home. It was divided into two parts; the story of Turu and the creation of the world, and a section on spells, both good and bad, depending on the point of view of those who invoked them. He opened to the page with the image of the Tree of Life. Beneath were the words he had read earlier, then lines of verse.

The Boughs of Turu

Atop the Crown of Heaven,
He rocked in the limbs of Turu;
Baptized in moonshine
And fed on the rays of the sun,
At the time when Earth had first begun

The son of simurghs melding
Waited for their nod,
Then bid goodbye to his home in the sky,
Stepped off the nest with arms outstretched
And flew down the beams of the moon

He walked the path of a human being
Before the word was penned,
The planet spoke beneath his feet,
He heard the rocks speak
And the voice in the wind

He didn't count his days on earth,
But in time his sheath grew weak
His powers waned as the wind blew cold
And the drums played a solemn beat

Returning to the mountain, straining with finger and toe,
He settled his mind and began the journey
To the bones in the valley below
Without a worry, without a care,
He leapt from the rocks and into the air

How long he fell, he didn't know;
Didn't count the eons pass
The wind blew him clean
And he woke from his dream,
Back in the boughs of Turu

The second half of the book was filled with incantations, execrations, and rites. There were incantations to cast out demons. Incantations to cast out disease, to make one invulnerable in battle, to win a lover, and for rain and good crops.

He skimmed through until he came to talismans. There was a large body of text devoted to stones and bones. A magic bone was described that had the power to send the possessor through a magic portal to other worlds. It told of the words to use to send enemies through the hole in the bone to the other realms. Like all the knowledge contained in the book, good or evil use depended on the perspective of the one using it. There were admonishments to use caution and to abide by the principals set forth in the story of creation.

There were incantations for restoring soul fragments to wholeness. Nick pondered on the meaning of 'soul fragment,' and realized that could be him. He did not feel complete in the modern world and had always felt pulled back to the past. Perhaps he could be whole again if he reunited with the lost parts of his being.

When coming to a set of tablets telling how to release souls from bondage, he became so absorbed he lost all sense of time. There were warnings to follow the ritual precisely and to concentrate on the meaning of the words. Any wavering or loss of determination could result in the sorcerer releasing their own soul into subjugation by the enslaver.

A growl escaped from the pit of Nick's stomach. It was nearly midnight and too late to eat dinner. As he climbed into bed, he resolved to pick up a bottle of eye drops for his burning eyes.

Chapter Fourteen:

Agatha Hensley

Nick walked up to Michael's desk and slumped down in the chair with a cup of coffee in his hand. His eyes looked like roadmaps.

Michael looked up in surprise. "I haven't seen you since Friday afternoon. Did you get snowed in somewhere?"

Nick blinked several times in succession. "No, I've been reading all weekend."

"You better get glasses. Your eyes are all red – or have you been smoking something illegal?"

Nick took a gulp from his cup. "I went to the university library to research congs and ran into Henryk Krauser. He gave me a book of Tocharian scripts he discovered at Bezeklik. They contain the myths of creation from the time of Shamadù. I can't put it down."

"Krauser? I wonder if the police … " The phone on his

desk rang. " … spoke to him." Michael answered, and a smile spread across his face. "Yes. I miss you, too." He took on a serious demeanor. "No. It can't be … describe it. Who? What's her number? Where?" He wrote down a name, address, and phone number on a Post-It. "The stone chime has been found."

Nick straightened up in his seat. "Who, what, where? What's going on?"

"Ann Lee is in Hong Kong setting up her art to sell at the Agatha Hensley Asian art auction. Hensley is putting up a stone chime for auction on Wednesday. Ann Lee wondered if it was our stone chime and described it perfectly."

"So, if we find who is selling it, we may have our thief?"

Michael shook his head. "Hensley is the Sotheby's of Asian art. Her reputation is impeccable. Art thieves are usually several links higher in the chain. I'm contacting the Hong Kong police and sending Xue to verify the piece is ours."

Xue arrived at the auction house on Queen's Way at closing time the day before the auction. There was no time to pick up his suit from the cleaners before leaving on the nine-hour flight. He introduced himself to Agatha Hensley wearing blue jeans and an old Nehru shirt. Although British, she had lived in Hong Kong since her marriage and chose to remain after the death of her husband. Acquiring her husband's estate by survivorship, she sold off much of his vast art collection and established her own auction house not far from the waterfront.

Ann Lee had returned to her hotel when Xue got there,

and the employee who answered the door told him he would have to come back in the morning to see Mrs. Hensley. Xue handed him his business card and explained that it was a matter of urgent importance. He was directed through the foyer to the main gallery where Agatha Hensley was making some adjustments to the auctioneer's catalogue.

She put the catalogue down beside an ancient cloisonné vase. "I'm afraid you have caught me at a bad time, Dr. Zhang. We had our preview today, and I must get in some last-minute changes for tomorrow. What can I do for you?"

"I apologize. I came right from the airport. I am here representing the Urumqi Regional Museum on an urgent matter. We believe you may have an artifact in your gallery that is stolen from the museum."

She regarded him with an inscrutable cold stare. "Are you accusing me of dealing black market art?"

Xue avoided her eyes. "No. No madam. You may be a victim of fraud."

"Before we go any further, what the hell are we talking about?"

"A stone chime from the Xia dynasty." He opened the dossier he had brought with him and handed her a museum catalogue sheet with a photo of the chime.

Hensley picked up the catalogue and thumbed through several pages. "Item number five." She led him over to a table closer to the auctioneer's podium.

"Xièxiè," said Xue, bowing. "This is it."

Agatha Hensley's eyes wrinkled. "Bùyòng xiè." She bowed her head slightly.

Xue pulled out descriptions of the missing Gu set pieces from the dossier. "Have you seen these items? They were stolen, too."

"No. But there is a different Gu piece from the same seller." She flipped the page to item number eleven. The description read 'Xinjiang Pottery Vessel, 3500 years old. Seller: a gentleman collector.'

"A jiao pottery vessel," said Xue. "It is part of the same set, but we could not find it at the excavation site. There is only one known complete set in existence."

She shook her finger at Xue. "You know what this means? One of *your* people is selling on the black market!"

Xue nodded in agreement. "We have suspected it. The police are on it, but have turned up nothing. Can you tell me who your seller is?"

Hensley scowled indignantly. "Not a chance. We only reveal the seller's name to the buyer, and no one else. This is an important client who has spent thousands and presented certificates of authenticity. I have legal obligations to my clients that I take seriously."

"Well, I am so grateful just to have recovered the chime. Do you have a shipping container for it?" He leaned toward the chime to pick it up.

"Just a moment. You don't think I can let you walk out with that, do you?"

"I'm sure you will only enhance your impeccable reputation by cooperating with the museum, Mrs. Hensley."

She took a deep breath and shook her head slowly. "I will release anything in question to the police, and to them only."

"You are wise, Mrs. Hensley. But please, don't put these on the block. I will return before then."

She nodded reluctantly and walked him to the door. "Tomorrow at nine."

Immediately upon leaving, Xue called Michael to let him know the stone chime was found. Michael was not as happy as Xue expected him to be, and was fearful that legal procedures could entangle its return to the museum since money had traded hands already and certificates of authenticity had been issued. It was too late to change the course of action. Michael informed Ann Lee and the Hong Kong detective bureau of the new developments.

The next morning Inspector Li from the police bureau spotted Xue waiting by the front door of the auction house and introduced himself. The auction wouldn't begin until ten, but many people had arrived early and were milling about inside. Xue and the inspector found their way to Agatha Hensley's office in a room at the back of the auction gallery. Ann Lee rose from her chair when they entered. "Good to see you, Xue."

Xue bowed politely. "Ann Lee, we are indebted to you for alerting us." He introduced the inspector to Mrs. Hensley and Ann Lee. The inspector produced a badge and held it out for everyone to see.

"I must be blunt, Inspector Li," said Agatha Hensley. "If it becomes known the police are here, some people may not even bid. My business could be ruined just by your presence. I would like this to be over with quickly."

"I understand, Mrs. Hensley. I don't want to cause any alarm." He looked at two boxes on her desk. "Are these the works in question?" The inspector opened the lids and peered inside.

"They are. I withdrew them from the auction as Dr. Zhang requested."

"Will the seller be coming to the auction?"

"No. He is overseas."

The inspector pursed his lips. "I will need the consignment papers and the certificates, please."

Agatha Hensley had anticipated this request beforehand and produced the signed originals from her desk drawer. "You can have them. I have copies."

"Thank you." He looked them over quickly. "These are in good order. The seller is a prominent person and has paid a handsome sum. Dr. Zhang, may I see those catalogue sheets and photos from the museum?"

Xue handed him the dossier. "It's all in there. Who is the seller?"

Inspector Li ignored him and grunted as he read over a letter explaining how the museum had unearthed the ancient art from the desert and recorded their discovery. He examined the museum catalogue sheets, then his eyes darted around the room from face to face. "Bad news – for everyone, I'm afraid. In order to return the art, we must prove there is a theft, but the thief has been clever and covered their tracks with a proof of ownership. The court will have to make a decision on this. We must impound the art and the paperwork until we catch the thief or until we can prove there has been a crime. It could take some time."

Xue and Ann Lee exchanged looks. "Inspector, let me take them back to the museum until you get it sorted out," said Xue.

"I'm sorry," said Inspector Li. He shut the lids on the boxes and collected the paperwork in the dossier to take with him.

"There's another way," said Ann Lee. "The knock-out bid. The museum can buy them back." She turned to the inspector with a frown. "Since the paperwork is so proper."

"It would save us much trouble if it is to our mutual benefit," said Inspector Li.

"And what is the price?" asked Xue.

Agatha Hensley handed him the catalogue. "Four times the reserve."

Xue looked at Ann Lee. "Maybe we'll will get lucky if I just bid." He rose and opened the door and peered into the main gallery. Five handlers stood by the podium pulling on white gloves. The auctioneer announced they were about to begin.

Agatha Hensley regarded Xue with a look of pity. "Dr. Zhang, people do not get lucky at my auction."

Xue smacked his forehead. "Yě shì zuì le."

"Use the back entrance," said Agatha Hensley.

Ann Lee led the two men to the rear door and let them out. "You did all you could, Xue," she said, locking the door behind them.

Chapter Fifteen:

Preparation for Departure

MICHAEL FUMBLED WITH THE switch of his desk lamp. "There is nothing we can do but wait."

"It's all backwards," said Nick. "We're the victims and we have to prove we're not the crooks. When is Xue going to get back?"

"He'll get in late Friday. We still have two hours before opening. Why don't you work with the display department to prepare for The Lost City tour. The mummies are going too, and you are familiar with them."

"That's actually perfect. I came across a talisman in the book Henryk Krauser gave me. It appears to be similar to the one in the male mummy's pouch in the mummy wing. I'd like to remove it from the display for a few days to study it and perhaps write it up to include in the exhibit."

Michael handed him a museum Receipt of Object form. "Great idea. Fill this out."

Nick joined Zeng and two handlers in the mummy gallery. Zeng had obtained the key to open Tok Ma's display case and was removing the lid. "Good, you are here, Nick. These are my handlers; Abliz Orkhun and Ömär Dawut."

"Es salaam aleikum," said Nick.

"Wa aleikum es salaam," they replied.

"What's the plan, Zeng?"

Abliz and Ömär helped Zeng set the lid on a cart. "It was relatively easy getting them here to the museum," he replied. "A world tour is another matter. There is a lot of legislation regarding the transport of the dead. I've done most of the customs and carrier notifications already. Today we are taking measurements to build the handling boards the mummies will rest on and crates for transport to the U.S. The museums where everything is going have environments that are compatible with ours, but we must build crates that have humidity control and are pest-proof to get them there. The corpses must be fully supported to prevent crushing or breakage."

The handlers measured the base and sides of the display case, then Zeng handed Nick a tape measure. "You aren't uncomfortable with touching him, are you?"

Nick smiled. "Not at all. We're old friends. And after thirty-eight hundred years, he's germ-free."

"He's more worried about your germs," said Zeng, holding out a pair of latex gloves and a gauze mask for Nick to put on. Zeng read from a list of body points requiring support during transport and Nick called them out as he took the measurements.

Nick gave the distance beneath Tok Ma's knees to the display bed, then handed back the tape. He held up the receipt signed by Michael. "One more thing, Zeng. I'm taking a talisman out of the pouch to do some research. You're my witness." He pulled back the waist flap of Tok Ma's coat and removed the bone from the pouch.

"An oracle bone?" asked Zeng.

"No. It's a human rib. But it does do time travel."

Zeng laughed. "Could it help me find my socks? My wife says socks go back in time when they are run in the dryer. It's because the drum spins counterclockwise without going anywhere and distorts the space time continuum, sending them back in time."

A smile, hidden by the mask, flickered across Nick's lips. "I'll look for your socks the next time I go back." He put the bone in a padded box, then helped the handlers return the display lid and lock it.

On their way back to the staff area, Zeng explained to Nick that Abliz and Ömär were going to begin building the crates. "When they're done, we'll start on the handling boards and I'll give you a call."

Back at his desk, Nick opened *The Book of Turu* and laid the bone beside it. The bone described in the texts as The Wizard's Bone appeared to be the same as Tok Ma's. Nick examined it more closely. There were heat cracks around the hole that resembled the hieroglyphic-like characters of ox bones used in prognostication, but this was a human rib bone, polished and smooth. According to the book, it was used to move either the living or the dead between worlds.

He began to sound out syllables of the Tocharian text and wrote down the translation on a note pad. Gail heard him through her open door across the hallway. She walked in and stood beside him, peering down at the book. "I thought you were talking to yourself."

Nick looked up with a smile. "Just practicing my Tocharian. Take a look at this. The bone from my friend Tok Ma's pouch is the same one in this book Krauser gave me."

"Wow. How cool is that. Can you translate it?"

"I'm working on it." Nick continued sounding out the words: "Wawuräs el poräswär mäntmne āsām, sam kpaśśäl wlaluneyis kälayme kaskal wrasom kuaprene, yomnās lame yātluneyo sne ñäktaśśi käm nā." He scratched his head. "Something like: by these words he will be sent through into the – um – belly – of the bird to be consumed by its fires."

"Sounds like an incantation."

He nodded. "Absolutely. *The Book of Turu* is filled with them."

Gail paged through the prints. "This is amazing. Are you working with Krauser on this? Where did he find the tablets?"

"Bezeklik. In some new caves they discovered there. He's

been teaching me Tocharian. Actually, pre-Tocharian. Much of it is speculation and guess work."

Her eyes softened. "Do you remember the Blue Baby – when we looked at it for the first time together? This reminds me of that moment. Sharing a discovery – together."

His eyes met hers. "That's when I realized we were on the same journey. We're sharing the same bliss."

"You do feel something for me then, don't you?" They regarded one another silently. "You don't have to love me, Nick. I have enough for two people. I know I'm not the girl in your poem, but maybe someday you'll wake up, and I want to be the one holding you."

He turned away. "I don't want to hurt you."

Gail looked up at the security camera in the ceiling. "Next Friday is my last day. I hope they don't have good-bye luncheons like they do in the states."

"I don't know. I only know I'll miss you...." He stood and walked to the far corner of the room just beneath the blind spot of the camera and motioned to her. Their lips lingered together for a moment, then she pushed herself away.

"I love you, Gail," he whispered as she walked out the door.

❧

Nick spent all the time he could devote to learning the incantations for releasing souls and casting enemies through the portal. He visited Henryk Krauser several times that week.

Every time he did, it snowed. And every time he rehearsed the words under the professor's tutelage, he felt a mysterious invigorating flow of energy course through him.

After several evenings of practice, the professor gave Nick praise for the advances he had made. "You have come a long way, Nick," he said. "I can teach you no more."

"Thank you, but I'll never know more than a pittance of what you do."

The professor gave Nick a pat on the back. "You know enough to put what you've learned to good use. My advice is to keep the bone close by. What you have learned won't work without it."

"I thought I was learning Tocharian. What do you mean?"

"Surely you have noticed the snow?"

"What does that have to do with anything?"

The professor smiled patiently. "Surely you have noticed the energy? When you learn and grow in your powers, the energy grows around you. Your power has grown. The sky and the earth are opposite energy fields that seek equilibrium, but the energy you give off disrupts the balance and …"

"Snow?"

The professor nodded. He held up his hand palm outward and *The Book of Turu* flew from the desk and hovered over it. He grasped the book firmly. "Take it from me."

Nick's jaw dropped. He reached out.

"No. It's simple. Know it is in your hand. Hold out your hand and see it there."

Nick closed his eyes and visualized it lying in his hand. Suddenly the book lay in his hand.

Henryk nodded. "You are ready, but none too soon. The storm is descending."

Nick heard snowflakes tapping forcefully on glass and walked to the window. It had grown late and the light from the campus lamps was unable to penetrate more than a few feet through the dense falling snow. "I am remembering more. I know what I must do, but I don't know where or how it will happen."

"It will start very soon, then you will find out and know what to do. Do you have the bone in your possession now?"

Nick turned and faced the professor. "I do."

"May I see it?" The professor saw the look of indecision on Nick's face and walked over to the window. "Surely you trust me by now."

Nick pulled a velvet bag from his coat pocket and removed the bone.

Henryk held it up and examined the cracks around the opening. He smiled sadly and handed it back. "Have a safe journey, friend. Goodbye."

Nick bowed his head. "Goodbye, Professor."

The snow was accumulating rapidly and swirled about his feet as he made his way to the car. When he got to his apartment building the street had just been plowed and his parking place was blocked by a two-foot-high pile of snow. He got out and made sure no one was looking. Holding out his hands over the car, he visualized it parked against the curb. *I could get used to it*, he said to himself.

There were puddles in the shape of footsteps leading through the lobby into the elevator. When he reached his floor he looked down the hall to his apartment where Gail lay in the fetal position against his door. "My God, are you alright?" he cried. He leaned down and shook her shoulder.

Gail uncurled and slowly stood up. "I was really cold. I must have fallen asleep."

"Come on inside." He put a kettle on the stove to make tea. "Take off your things."

"I wish you had a cell phone. I came over because we have a problem at the tomb."

"Couldn't it have waited until tomorrow?" He hung her coat and hat on a chair and pushed it near the radiator to dry. "What's up?"

Gail rubbed her hands together. "I examined a set of satellite scans of the base of the mountain where the tunnel to the tomb is supposed to be. There are nine looting holes with tire tracks all around them."

"Are these new scans?"

"Taken yesterday. Do you think they found the tomb?"

"Yes. Nine holes is a lot. They kept guessing for nine tries until they found the tunnel. They were pretty sure they were on to something. Oh man! It's someone from the excavation." Nick slumped down at the table and massaged his temples. "Did you notify the police down there?"

"Michael called them and talked to the security guards at the camp. At least the funerary chamber is secure."

The kettle began whistling and Nick got up to make a pot of tea. The wind rattled the windows as he sat back down and poured. "We need to get down there right now, but with this blizzard we ain't going nowhere. It's funny. Henryk Krauser said a storm was descending. He wasn't talking about the blizzard, though."

"The consensus is that his elevator doesn't go all the way up."

"He knows plenty. I've learned a lot from him."

Gail smiled. "I guess he has some redeeming features. Not to change the subject, but I can't go out there. Can I stay here tonight?"

Nick blew on his tea thoughtfully and smiled. "I can sleep on the sofa. You can have my bed."

"Oh no. I'm not going to miss out on an opportunity like a blizzard. We need to keep each other warm."

"Sure?"

"Positively."

They decided to dig out early in the morning to get to the museum, then retired to bed early without finishing their tea. After undressing one another, they climbed into bed and made love as the snow pattered against the windows.

He traced the shape of her breasts with his fingers, slowly traveling down to her stomach and navel. "I'm getting lost. I'll have to make a map." He ran the side of his hand toward her stomach. "A river flows from the peaks and into the valley below. It fills a basin here, and here is a beautiful smooth lake," he whispered, kissing her stomach. When they were done their love making, eddies of pleasure whorled them into sleep.

Nick awoke when a gust of wind rattled the bedroom window. He shifted onto his side and watched her sleeping. "I know you think I don't love you. You're wrong."

Chapter Sixteen:

Sludge

"How much did we get?" Gail asked.

Nick fastened his robe and walked to the window. It looked bitterly cold, but the wind had stopped and the sun was shining. "About a foot. Looks like a foot and a half out there altogether."

She wrapped the bedspread around her and followed him into the kitchen. "What do you want for breakfast?" he asked, rummaging through the cabinets one at a time. "You can have anything you want as long as it's oatmeal.

"Do you have coffee?"

Nick shook his head. "Chai. I have some nang bread fresh out of the tannur yesterday. It's better right out of the oven, but I can heat it."

She sat down by the stove. "That sounds great."

He bent down and kissed her on the forehead. "Thanks for

your patience. Comin' right up." A few minutes later, he set the Chai on the table and broke off a warm piece of nang and handed it to her.

"How are we going to get down to Shamadù?" she asked. "It's going to take a long time to dig out from all this."

Nick lifted up Tok Ma's pouch sitting by *The Book of Turu.* "There is a way. It's kind of like travelling through a worm hole."

"I don't want to end up in an alternate reality. No thanks. I'll take something more conventional. We're going to need to bring the police in on this, too."

Nick sighed wistfully. "I doubt the museum will be open today. There aren't any landline phones in this building, either. Let's try to Skype Michael. If that doesn't work, I think we need to go to the museum and hope he makes it in."

When they had eaten, Nick tried to connect with Skype, first to Michael, then to Xue, but there was no response. "The Rover is good in the snow. Are you ready?" he asked.

Gail felt her clothes on the back of the chair to see if they were dry. She nodded resolutely. "Give me a couple of minutes."

Nick grabbed his knapsack and placed *The Book of Turu* and the pouch inside. After insulating himself against the cold with his heaviest coat and gloves, he crammed his Uyghur hat on his head.

Gail emerged from the bedroom. "Let's do it."

Outside, the sidewalk and road were empty. Nick brushed the snow from the windows of the Land Rover and started the engine. He shifted the vehicle into four-wheel drive and rocked it back and forth until he was out in the street, then headed for the museum. The unplowed snow made the going difficult.

"We'll have to get a weather report for the south," said Gail. "We're not going to make it if the roads are like this all the way."

The vehicle slid sideways toward a snow bank and came to a stop. Nick twisted around in the seat and backed up to the other side of the street. "There shouldn't be more than a dusting near the base of the mountain," he said as they resumed their way. "They don't get much snow down there, but at this rate, we won't even make it out of town."

An hour later they arrived at the front parking lot of the museum. "It's closed," said Gail. "Not one set of tire tracks."

"Let's drive around back," Nick replied. He navigated by way of lamp poles and parking signs to the rear staff entrance. Two museum police cars with snow drifts covering the hoods were parked alongside the emergency power generator. Nick pointed to the snowbound cars and grimaced as he and Gail made their way to the entrance past the roar of the generator.

"Must be Wang and Alim," said Gail, pulling the door shut behind them. "They probably spent the night."

"I think you're right." They proceeded along the corridor, lit only by the emergency lighting, toward the security office. As they neared, Alim stepped out into the hall. "Gail? Who's with you?" he asked, squinting.

"It's just Nick and me," she replied.

"Come in." Alim motioned them into the office.

Wang was studying the Urumqi power grid on a wall display. "We're on emergency power," he said. "Half the town got knocked out. Michael and Xue live in the affected area."

"How are the roads outside of Urumqi?" asked Gail.

"No good," said Wang. "Everything's shut down for three hundred miles. It's not bad down in the far south, from what I can tell."

"What's the word on the looting holes? Did the local police make it out to take a look?" asked Nick.

Wang shook his head. "They wanted to meet with a museum official before going in. It's a national protected site. They must be accompanied by someone who is qualified to assess and safeguard the artifacts."

"That's not good," said Nick. "The tomb could be emptied out by now. We have to get down there."

Wang held his finger in the air imperiously. "There is some good news. I informed Inspector Li in Hong Kong of the discovery of the looting holes, and he has brought in the Urumqi police to collaborate on our case. They asked for us to accompany them to the site, but Alim and I must stay here. Can you go with them to Shamadù, Nick?"

"I'd be delighted."

"I'm going, too," said Gail.

"But don't you have to fly back to the States in two days?" asked Nick.

"I'll cancel my flight."

Nick looked at Wang imploringly. "It could be dangerous, right, Wang?"

Wang nodded. "We don't know what to expect. It could be."

"How often do you actually catch a looter, Wang?" Gail folded her arms and stared at Wang. "I have as much invested in this project as anyone else. I'm not asking permission. I'm going."

They watched the police helicopter set down through the museum's rear security cameras. Wang unlocked a desk drawer and handed a holstered pistol to Nick. "Just in case," he said. "It's loaded."

Nick shook his head and handed it back. "No thanks."

"It's your decision," said Wang. He motioned the gun toward Gail and raised his eyebrows inquisitively.

"I know how to shoot a gun, but thanks for asking."

He put it back in the drawer. "But you must take this." He handed her a museum cell phone. "Keep me updated."

"Okay, Wang." She opened Nick's knapsack and placed the phone on top the *Book of Turu*. Fastening the top back down, she looked at Nick. "Are you going to be catching up on your Tocharian?"

Nick shrugged. "Maybe."

Alim walked with them to the back entrance and waved from the doorway. A plain clothesman jumped from the helicopter into the blinding updraft of snow and helped them in.

Once inside, he closed the door and the craft rose into the air. He pointed to their seatbelts. "Strap in," he ordered with a British accent. When they had picked up altitude and speed, he extended his hand. "Lieutenant Bill Hughes, Interpol."

"Albert Guo," said the pilot, raising his hand without looking up from the controls.

"Sergeant Guo, MSS," Hughes added.

"Just Albert is fine."

Hughes looked up in supplication. When the amenities had been observed, Nick leaned over Gail and shouted above the noise, "We thought the Urumqi police were handling this."

"When Li contacted them about the chime showing up in Hong Kong, they realized this could be a lead into an international crime ring, so here we are."

"I'm glad you're on this, but I still don't get why. Don't the Chinese usually want to handle everything themselves?"

Hughes nodded. "Usually, but things in Hong Kong have gotten out of control and too political. We have a number of cases we're working on centered in Hong Kong with ties to Europe and South America."

"I understand," said Nick, "but how do we fit into this?"

"The problem is, when artifacts are stolen, they aren't usually registered. Tombs and temples are emptied before we even get there, and you don't know what you don't know."

"But our finds are documented."

"Exactly. In your case we've been able to trace the fellow putting it up on the auction block."

"No one will tell us anything. So, who is it?" asked Gail.

The lieutenant grimaced. "What the bloody fuck. Thomas Alcock." He waited for a reaction.

"The name doesn't mean anything to me," said Nick. "Me either," said Gail.

"We know the goods originated at your dig, were stolen from the museum, then sold to Thomas Alcock. He's part of a money laundering ring. Alcock typically buys up real estate … penthouse suites and residential buildings … in South America. It's harder to trace the money if it's converted into property. The thief and Alcock are part of the same ring. They buy their own stolen art on paper without spending a cent, resell it at auctions or to gentleman collectors, then hide the profits in real estate."

"They just sell off a building every now then if they need a little cash," said Gail with a wry smile.

Hughes let out a laugh. "Yeah. Something like that."

Talk was difficult in the noisy aircraft and they lapsed into silence. A few hours later they began descending and landed at an oilfield heliport in the middle of the Taklamakan desert.

"Pitstop," said Albert. He flipped off several toggle switches and removed the key from the console lock. "Stretch your legs and come right back. We'll be underway again as soon as we refuel."

"Nick, why did you bring the talisman?" asked Gail when they were alone.

He pulled Tok Ma's pouch out of the knapsack and removed the bone. "It's complicated. It's not just about stopping the bad guys from stealing ancient art from the rest of the world. There's some unfinished business that needs to be taken care of." He ran his fingers over the polished surface.

"You've been spending too much time in the library. Krauser is playing some sort of game with you. He's nuts."

Nick looked into her eyes imploringly. "It's not a game. There is something calling me from the past. I have a family… and a place where I belong … nearly four thousand years ago in the past. Until I get back, I'm a soul fragment. There is a sacred charge to be fulfilled, and if I don't, I have failed and can't be complete. It sounds crazy, but now is the time to fulfil it … with this." He closed his eyes and held up Tok Ma's bone reverently, offering it to some invisible force.

Gail shook her head. "Nick, you have to let go of that near-death experience."

Nick smiled mysteriously and put the bone back. "I'd feel the same way. I don't blame you for thinking that." A fuel truck pulled up and a worker began unwinding the hose. "I'm going to the hangar over there and take care of some other business."

When the refueling was complete the lieutenant stood by the aircraft and waited for Gail and Nick as the pilot ran over the preflight checklist. When everyone was onboard, Hughes twisted in his seat. "When we get there, we will only have about two more hours of daylight. Do you guys think that will give you enough time to assess the situation and take some photos before we find a place to stay the night in Shamadù?"

"We don't have much choice," said Nick as they took off. "It will have to do."

They flew for another hour and a half. The Kunlun grew larger with every passing minute and filled the horizon as they approached their destination. Albert dropped the craft lower and Nick could make out the Taklamakan Highway he had travelled when he first came to Shamadù. They passed over the highway and made their way to the base of the mountain where it merged into the frozen piedmont.

As they headed east, Nick spotted the Crown of Heaven. "Head into that fold at the base," he said, pointing with his finger. The looting holes swung into view: nine random holes, each about three meters wide, set in an irregular pattern along the sides of bulldozer tracks.

As they approached the holes, the helicopter began its descent in a long spiral. "Those tracks are heading toward Niya," said Hughes.

"Should we see where they go?" asked Albert.

"No. Let's land down by the middle one. Looks like signs of activity there. We can check out the tracks later."

The craft set down about thirty yards from the hole. Hughes walked over cautiously and peered down, then motioned for the others to follow. The pilot dragged a supply chest from the back of the helicopter and slid it over the ground. Nick grabbed a handle and helped pull it to the hole. Inside were flashlights and ropes and rappelling gear.

Gail pulled her camera from her coat pocket and took pictures of the closest holes, then pointed to bulldozer tracks skirting the farthermost hole in the direction of the desert. "That looks like a cave-in." The ground had sunken several feet and the earth had been torn and gouged by the track shoes as the machine fought its way out of the depression.

"What do we have down there?" asked Lieutenant Hughes. "We're not stepping into a pile of poo, are we? Is that cave-in part of the tomb?"

"A pile of Xie Pu," said Nick. He pointed in the direction of The Lost City and traced the path of the tunnel with his finger through the air to the base of the Kunlun. "It's all tunnel through these looting holes. Then it enters Xie Pu's funerary chambers at the base of the mountain."

Hughes bent down over the chest and dug out several flashlights, then handed them out to the others. "Just what is it that made them go to all this trouble?"

Nick put his arms through the shoulder straps of his back-pack and slid it on his back. "Xie Pu wasn't what you would call an enlightened ruler. A lifetime of hoarded treasure is buried down there along with him. We don't even know how much it's worth in today's money. They never make it easy ... it's going to be dangerous. I suggest Gail and Albert stay up here to stand guard. You and I can go down and get the pictures you need. I got to check on something down there."

Hughes's eyebrows narrowed. "What's that?"

"I have to find his sepulcher and verify it's really him down there."

"Everything he told you is theory, Lieutenant," said Gail. "What he really wants is to get credit for the discovery. I'm going with you, Nick."

Hughes shook his finger at them. "Having a bit of a spat, are we? We're all going together."

Albert pulled a long coil of rope from the chest and handed it to the lieutenant who walked to the lip of the looting hole. Setting the coil down, he reached into his coat pocket and removed a plastic bag and a pair of tweezers. Picking up a cigarette butt with the tweezers, he held it to his nose and sniffed.

"Camels, I'd say," he remarked, and dropped it into the bag. "I smoked these when I was a kid." He smiled wryly. "It was a rough neighborhood."

"Chang smokes them," said Gail.

Hughes straightened up and threw the end of the rope to Albert. "Drive a stake in and tie us up, Albert."

"The ground's too soft," Nick broke in. "Better tie up to the chopper." Albert grunted and tied the end to a landing strut.

"Who's Chang?" asked Hughes.

"Jih-Wen Chang," said Nick. "You could say he is the straw

boss of the excavators. He's been around digs for a long time. If there's such a thing as an indispensable person, then he is it."

"Interesting," said Hughes. He stuffed the specimen in his pocket and threw the remaining coils of rope down the hole. "A little soon to start speculating. Here we go." He switched on his flashlight and inserted it into the headband of his hat and began rappelling down the shaft.

The other three peered over the edge and watched as Hughes descended. When he reached the floor of the tunnel he turned around slowly in a circle. Looking upward, he signaled the others to come down.

"How's the air down there?" asked Nick.

"A bit like rotten eggs, but not too bad," he replied.

Nick climbed over the edge and looped the rope around one foot, then lowered himself quickly to the bottom. He held the rope out from the side of the shaft for Gail and Albert.

When they had landed, they guided their flashlight beams along the walls and floor. The looting hole shaft had pierced through the ceiling to one side of the tunnel. The seven-meter-deep shaft had been dug by using small charges of explosives to break up the rocks and soil, then carting the debris away to the surface. There had been a cave-in a short distance to the left of them from the weight of a bulldozer passing overhead, sealing the tunnel completely. Swinging their flashlight beams in the other direction, the light faded into darkness about ninety meters down the tunnel.

Gail took photos of the walls and ceiling. The ceiling was made of thick planks coffered with heavy supporting beams. The walls were rammed earth similar to those in the funerary chamber and were decorated with monster heads. Torches, the fuel consumed millenniums ago, were placed at regular intervals. The floor was a polished red marble covered in a deep layer of dust. Footprints made their way in both directions along the length of the tunnel.

Hughes knelt beside the tracks and took several photos. "There are four sets going in, and three coming back. They were running back to the shaft, judging by the length of their strides."

"Something must have scared them," said the pilot.

"Chang wasn't the type to get scared," Nick replied.

Hughes stood up wearing a frown. "Let's not draw any conclusions."

"Come on, it's getting late." Nick aimed his beam into the darkness. "There's only one way to go. Follow the red dragon road."

Hughes and Guo were still far behind when Gail caught up to Nick. "We don't know it's Chang," she said. She lowered her voice. "Why are you walking so fast?"

"Somethings are intuitively obvious." A rumble was heard coming from the area of the cave-in. He glared at Gail with popping eyes and broke into a run. "I have a bad feeling about this. Hurry!"

"Jesus, Nick, come on." Her effort to keep up caused her to pant in the sour air.

The rumbling grew closer and cracks spread in the ceiling near the shaft where they had entered. Nick stopped abruptly and turned around, cupping his hands to his mouth. "Run!"

Hughes shined his flashlight back toward the looting hole shaft. Albert was slipping on the floor in a rapidly spreading pool of bituminous liquid pouring through the rubble. He got to his feet and convulsed in spasms of tortured coughing. Stumbling to the rope, he attempted to pull himself up, but his hands and feet were covered in the thick tar. He drew a deep breath, then fell back to the floor and lay still. In the moment Hughes contemplated rescuing his associate, the ceiling above his head split open and a thick stream of bitumen and tar sand spilled downward.

"Come on!" screamed Gail. Hughes lurched down the tunnel toward her gasping and coughing. Nick and Gail ran back to meet him halfway, then each put an arm beneath a shoulder and dragged him forward.

As Hughes began to recover some of his strength, they stood him against the side of the tunnel and Nick directed the beam of his flashlight into his face. "Are you okay?" asked Nick. The lieutenant's eyes were red and swollen and his face was pale.

Hughes shook his head weakly. "I guess. What the hell is that stuff?"

"Tar sand and bitumen," said Nick. "It could be seepage from an oil field. I don't know if it's a booby trap or if it's occurring naturally. It's too bad about Albert, but there's nothing we can do now."

"It's toxic, that's for sure," said Gail. "How are we going to get out of here?"

They watched as the sludge continued its way toward them. "There has to be a system of drains leading to the outside to prevent flooding," said Nick. "We'll have to keep our eyes open."

"It's getting close," said Gail. "Are you ready, Lieutenant?"

Hughes forced himself up straight. "Yeah. Lead on."

Hughes continued to cough periodically but was able to keep up the fast pace as they made their way to the dark end of the tunnel. The distance from the black sludge began to increase.

"We're going upward, now," said Nick. "We must be under the mountain. The legend says the Kunlun is filled with caverns." The darkness continued for several minutes until a faint shimmer manifested itself in the distance. "Do you see something ahead?"

Chapter Seventeen:

The Caverns of Kunlun

THE FLOOR OF THE tunnel continued to arc upward, and the sides and height expanded in proportion with the incline. The glimmer they had noticed proved to be the lower portion of a door that increased in height as they neared it. The door, encrusted with jewels that sparkled in the twilight, was set into a wall of white marble blocks that rose to the top of an enormous cavern, preventing further egress into the hollows of the mountain.

Gail and Hughes took photographs as Nick examined the door. He still hadn't been able to open it when they joined him. Gail pushed down on a rearing cobra head. A click was heard on the inside.

"She's brilliant," said Hughes. He pushed until it opened enough for them to squeeze through. Before them was a cavern vaster than the first. Stalagmites and stalactites glistened to create an underworld cathedral. The sound of a subterranean stream played musically in the background. A soft wavering light played over the cavern walls in time to the music of the flowing water. Three doors similar to the first one they had passed were set into the cavern wall on the far side.

"I don't think we need our flashlights," Nick said with reverence. He turned his off, and the others followed suit. The belly of the mountain glowed with a supernatural light.

"It's beautiful," said Gail. "I could stay here forever."

"Don't be deceived. We're in great danger," Nick replied. He ran to the source of the light and looked into a watercourse hewn into the rock. As the sun set outside, its rays struck the subterranean stream cascading from the side of the mountain and traveled back through the water to illuminate the cavern. He closed his eyes and traveled to the time he crawled through tall grass at the base of the Crown of Heaven wearing a hooded cloak. The mountain towered above him. A waterfall spilled from the side of the mountain into a pool of water and continued on across the plain.

Nick shook his head to clear it. "Get your pictures, then get the hell out through here." He pointed downward into the water.

Hughes jaw dropped. "You're insane. You couldn't live a minute in that water."

Nick slipped the knapsack from his back and pulled out the *Book of Turu* along with the pouch. He thumbed through the book then pointed to the door on the right. "Get your pictures."

Nick opened it, and the three of them entered a chamber filled with urns and piles of treasure. He reached into an urn and pulled out handfuls of blue stones and stuffed them in his coat pockets as Hughes and Gail took pictures.

"I saw you," said Hughes. "What's the difference between you and a looter?"

Nick shrugged. "Not much. But these are for something larger than just you or me. Trust me, it is larger, okay?"

Hughes scowled at Nick in disgust. "You're not who I thought you were. You're just like the rest of them." He took one last photo then stepped back through the door. "What's in that one?" He pointed to the middle door and pushed down on the latch.

"Don't go in there!" cried Nick as Hughes pushed the door open and entered.

"Piss up a rope, Jesus," said Hughes beneath his breath. The middle chamber, lit by the waterborne light, stretched back as far as the eye could see. Thousands of shelves stacked four high were filled with the bones of the people of the Lost City of Shamadù. Lining the aisles were congs, one for each soul. Jih-Wen Chang lay on a marble table as two priestly specters drained the blood from his nearly lifeless body into the concave top of a cong. The souls of the dead emerged from the funerary containers as wisps of mist and murmured their protests against the living intruders. Gail followed Hughes inside and screamed as the wisps congregated in the air above them.

Hughes stepped backward and collided with Gail in the

doorway. The priests looked up as he unholstered his pistol and fired wildly in their direction. As they floated toward him through the bullets, one reached out its hand and into his chest. Hughes struggled for a moment then fell to the floor. The second priest advanced on Gail and reached out for her as she frantically tried to disentangle herself from the detective.

Nick put his arms around her and pulled her away, then held up the bone and recited from the book: "*Nek śaryam ñakta śaranne asteske mrestiweśc. Yem śarāmne pośaul nanmasa.*"

The murmur of the dead ceased. The cavern grew quiet. A whirling ring of fire emerged from the hole in the bone and expanded. Another appeared, followed by yet another. As the rings proliferated in the air, a cleansing wind blew through the cavern.

Gail turned to Nick. "I believe you," she said and wiped away the tears falling down his cheeks.

"It is almost done. There is one thing more," he replied.

The rings, coruscated with blue, white, and gold, drew the spirits to them and through the hole in the bone. "Let go of the chains that have held you here," said Nick. "You are free now." The apparitions disappeared inside them.

When the last soul had passed through, the rings extinguished. Gail bent down where Lieutenant Hughes lay and felt for his pulse. "He's gone," she said.

"I liked him," said Nick. He returned the bone to its pouch. "You're going to have to leave now. There is one more door to open, and if you stay, you will die."

"Wherever you are going, I want to go with you, Nick. Take me too."

"As much as I'd like to, that's not possible. Come." He took her hand and walked with her to the glowing stream. They embraced with eyes closed. "Love's not time's fool," he whispered in her ear.

"Shit, Nick. I'm not going to see you again, am I?"

"Not in this life." Nick brushed her cheek with his hand. "I have to go."

He returned to the third door and laid his hand on the latch, summoning all his energy and determination. Looking back, there was no sign of Gail. He pushed on the brass cobra head and entered. The burial chamber of Lord Xie Pu was of immense proportions and furnished with intricately carved tables and seats. Lifelike statues sat at the tables as though engaged in lively conversation.

Torches burned in tall braziers placed throughout the chamber. In the center was a raised floor of red dragon marble. Armored basalt soldiers surrounded an open jade sarcophagus in the middle. Nick wove his way around the still figures in the eerie light to the sarcophagus. Inside was the king's corpse adorned in a burial suit made of jade rectangles sewn together with copper wire, and over this, a piece of woven gold embroidered with lapis lazuli, amethyst, and sapphires.

The chamber showed no signs of having been disturbed over the millennia. Or perhaps the servants had just finished cleaning and putting everything back in perfect order. Nick bent over the sarcophagus and placed the blue stones inside. He opened the *Book of Turu*, looked down at the form of the king, and held up the bone. "Lord Xie Pu, awaken and arise," he commanded.

Jade-encrusted hands mechanically raised to the clasp that fastened the face piece and pulled the flap that covered Xie Pu's face to one side.

"Who dares disturb me from my sleep?" asked a voice from the blackness inside.

The face of the king took form and the arms pushed him into a sitting position. The form continued to rise then stepped onto the floor eye level with Nick. Lord Xie Pu regarded Nick for a moment and laughed. "I remember you. You are the fool they call Tok Ma. It seems you have outlasted me."

"It doesn't matter how I am called. The important thing is that I remember what you did to the people of Shamadù. They are free now, and you're going to hell where you belong."

A stone warrior pulled Gail across the floor by the hair. The basalt figures surrounding the king straightened to attention. "Let me go!"

Nicks eyes followed her as she kicked to free herself. "Why are you still here?" he demanded.

"I want to go with you." The warrior threw her down at the feet of Xie Pu.

Xie Pu laughed. "How devoted. I will eat both your souls anyway, and they will taste good. I haven't eaten in a long time. Guards, bring the congs."

Nick held up his hand to the guards, palm outward. "Chi!" he commanded and began incanting: "*Wawuräs el poräswär* ...." Xie Pu motioned to the warriors. They raised their lances to impale him.

Xie Pu pulled the bone from Nick's fingers. "It's been such a long time, but you haven't changed." He smirked derisively and turned it over in his hands to examine it, then peered through the hole inquisitively.

Nick calmly began the incantation again: "*Wawuräs el poräswär mäntmne āsām, sam kpaśśäl wlaluneyis kälayme kaskal wrasom kuaprene, yomnās lame yātluneyo sne ñäktaśśi käm nā.*"

Xie Pu staggered and threw down the bone. Gail picked it up and held it before him.

"Fenghuang!" cried Nick. "It is time."

The fire rings emerged from the hole once again. As they burst through and filled the air, Fenghuang stepped out of the last ring and clasped Xie Pu in a talon. The evil lord kicked and flailed as the warriors pricked the bird with their lances to no avail, then the simurgh bent down and swallowed him whole to assimilate in his belly.

Fenghuang turned to Nick. "It is done, my friend. What you do next is yours to decide."

The bird scooped up the blue stones in its beak and cooed. Hot licks of flame rippled across its wings as Fenghuang folded them into its body then disappeared into the rings.

As soon as Lord Xie Pu vanished down the gullet of the

bird, the warriors returned to stone. Ground tremors shook the cavern and cracks formed along the walls and ceiling.

Nick took the bone from Gail. "Thank you for what you did. It took a lot of courage."

"Don't thank me. Take me with you."

Another rumble shook the cavern. He shook his head. "The universe is returning to equilibrium. The energy released is beyond imagination. It's a good thing, but time has run out. Get out of here before it's too late."

Nick held up the bone. "*Wrakuaprene yomnās*." The rings surrounded him. "I'll always love you, Gail." He stepped into the vortex.

Gail looked into the whirling energy of the rings. She could make out a man wearing a maroon coat and tall deerskin boots on the back of the flaming simurgh flying over streets lined with rammed earth houses. The rings coalesced, and the portal closed.

She heard the sound of gurgling water and looked down at her feet. Water was streaming in through the doorway and across the floor. A falling block of marble jarred her back to consciousness of the imminent danger. She hastily splashed her way back to the subterranean stream. Several boulders had fallen into the waterway from above, diverting the flow onto the floor of the cavern, leaving only a trickle in the streambed. She lowered herself down and started running. The bed ran in a straight line for about forty meters where it exited the side of the mountain. Halfway down, she came to a deep pool. Grabbing at outcrops of rock overhead, she was able to climb around to safety. Constant tremors and falling rock impeded her progress, but at last she reached the point of egress.

The looting holes were about a kilometer away. Looking down the mountain to where the helicopter should be, she could barely make it out. The temperature had dropped considerably and was already well below freezing, but at least she was dry. The terrain was extremely rough and demanding.

It was long past dark by the time she got to the chopper. She turned on the police radio to request help, but Albert had the key to the electrical system. "Poor Albert," she said aloud. There was a pile of blankets for emergencies in the luggage compartment. She pulled out three and lay across the back seat and covered herself. The ground shook as she fell asleep, too tired to even notice.

❧

Through the fog of her exhaustion, she felt Michael's hand shake her shoulder. "Are you alright?" he asked. She sat up and looked out the window. It was the middle of the day. A police helicopter had landed nearby, and several policemen congregated at the looting hole.

"I'm freezing," she said.

"Walk around a little, you'll feel better," said Michael. He helped her out and walked with her. "Where's Nick?"

She shrugged her shoulders, unable to think of what to say. "It went wrong, terribly wrong."

"They found the pilot down the hole. When he didn't radio in, we got worried. Where's Lieutenant Hughes?"

She pointed to the mountain. "With Jih-Wen Chang. Dead."

Michael shook his head. "I'm going to have a talk with those fellows and see if we can get you back to Urumqi. You don't look so good." He guided Gail to the other chopper and motioned the pilot to come over.

Chapter Eighteen:

Farewell to Xinjiang

GAIL UNDERWENT SEVERAL INTERROGATIONS relating to Nick. Inspector Li questioned her the day before she left for Philadelphia. When she arrived at Urumqi police headquarters she was directed into an empty office. Inspector Li came in a few minutes later and sat down at the desk.

"Ms. Norton, this should not take long. We are trying to wrap this case up, but there are still some things that are not accounted for. I hope you can shed some light."

"I'll try, Inspector."

Li smiled pleasantly. "I understand you and Nick Taylor were close."

Gail shifted uneasily in her seat. "We were good friends."

"I know you think I'm prying, and you are right." He looked at her with the same pleasant smile. "There are some irregularities, and I am trying to determine to what extent you are trying to cover up for him."

"What do you mean, cover up for him?" *Don't blink so much*, she told herself.

"In your written statement, you said you were the only one to get out of the cave-in alive, and yet when we sent in the rescue team, there was no trace of Mr. Taylor. We recovered the bodies of the pilot, Guo, Jih-Wen Chang, and Lieutenant Hughes, but not Mr. Taylor. And the remains of that king that was supposed to be the reason for going in there in the first place ... nothing."

Gail sat stone-faced. "What are you implying, Inspector?"

"He's alive, isn't he? You and he escaped together. Nick Taylor had access to the storage room at the museum. Did he take the stone chime? Is he in league with Thomas Alcott? Was the cave-in his getaway?"

Gail struggled to maintain her composure. "I'm not covering up anything. I'm only trying to protect the reputation of a brilliant man. A great archaeologist who no one ... understood." *Don't shake your head. Don't blink.*

Inspector Li watched Gail dispassionately. "Give me an address and a phone number where we can reach you when you get back home. You can go."

෨

The police closed the investigation into the deaths of Jih-Wen Chang and detectives Guo and Hughes two weeks after the incident at the Crown of Heaven. They left Nick's case open as an unexplained disappearance. Opinion was divided. There were those who thought he and Chang were in it together as part of the art theft ring. That explained the access to the stolen objects required to steal the artifacts. On the other hand, if they accepted Gail's story, then it was simply a matter of Nick being buried so deeply in the rubble that his remains were unrecoverable.

After Gail was cleared to return to Philadelphia, she said her goodbyes to her friends at the museum. On her last day, she cleaned out her desk and decided to visit the mummy wing before taking a cab to the airport.

Tok Ma and his family lay in their display cases. She looked down at Tok Ma. "Nice boots," she said. "You guys are going to do some traveling soon."

"Maybe you'll see him in Philadelphia." Startled, Gail turned around to find Henryk Krauser standing behind her. "I'm going to be lecturing at the University of Pennsylvania when the mummies go on tour. Maybe I'll see you there, too?"

Gail smiled. "Professor, I owe you an apology. Nick said you knew a thing or two, and I didn't believe him. Now I know better."

"Apology accepted. So, maybe I'm not crazy after all?"

"He took the bone with him."

Krauser smiled wistfully. "It's in good hands."